TALE OF DRAGONFLY

BOOK I: LATE SUMMER TO AUTUMN

SHANE CURTIS FIKE, POLIA GIANNOULIDIS

NOX ARCANUM EXPERIMENT

TALE OF DRAGONFLY BOOK I: LATE SUMMER TO AUTUMN

COPYRIGHT © 2020, 2021 by Shane Curtis Fike

Cover design, illustration, and imagery by Polia Giannoulidis

COPYRIGHT © 2021 by Polia Giannoulidis, Shane Curtis Fike

The Library of Congress Cataloging-in-Publication Data is available upon request.

ISBN: 978-0-6451798-8-0

BOOKS PUBLISHED BY

Nox Arcanum Experiment

Tale of Dragonfly, *Book I: Late Summer to Autumn*
Tale of Dragonfly, *Book II: Autumn to Winter*
Tale of Dragonfly, *Book III: Winter to Spring*
Tale of Dragonfly, *Book IV: Spring to Summer*
The Raven's Daughter, *A Trickster's Creation Story*
Shadows of America, *Road to Authenticity*

Nox Arcanum Experiment

Embrace the mystery of you.

"The all is mind. The universe is mental; held in the mind of the all. All is in the all. To who truly understands this truth, hath come great knowledge." -Three Initiates

ACKNOWLEDGEMENT

The author and illustrator make no claim of legitimacy, affiliation or relation to any Indigenous identity or sovereign nation.

We stand on the lands of Indigenous peoples, whose ancestors have resided here since Time Immemorial. Many Indigenous peoples thrive in this place—alive and strong.

The life lessons brought about in Indigenous storytelling are essential for Indigenous peoples to make sense of the world and to teach about values, history, significant events, relationships, cultural beliefs, and sacred stories.

We understand that Land Acknowledgments have been used to start conversations regarding how non-Indigenous people can support Indigenous sovereignty and advocate for land repatriation; however, historical, and anthropological facts demonstrate that many contemporary land acknowledgments unintentionally communicate false ideas about the history of dispossession and the current realities of Indigenous peoples—those ideas have detrimental consequences for Indigenous peoples and nations.

No data exists to demonstrate that land acknowledgements lead to measurable, concrete change. Instead, they often serve as little more than feel-good public gestures signaling ideological conformity.

This is evident in the evocation in many acknowledgments of a time when Indigenous peoples acted as "stewards" or "custodians" of the land now occupied; along with related references, such as "ancestral homelands"—this relegates Indigenous peoples to a mythic past and fails to acknowledge that they owned the land. Even if unintentionally, such assertions tacitly affirm the putative right of non-Indigenous people to now claim title.

This is also implied in what goes unsaid. The implication is: "What was once yours is now ours."

Additionally, in most cases these statements fail to acknowledge the violent trauma of land being stolen from Indigenous people—the death, dispossession and displacement of countless individuals and much collective suffering. The afterlives of these traumas are deeply felt and experienced in Indigenous communities; but because non-Indigenous people are generally unaware of this trauma, land acknowledgments are often heard by Indigenous peoples as the denial of that trauma.

This perspective is reinforced by a tendency to cast Indigenous peoples as part of prehistory, suggesting that the trauma of dispossession, if it happened at all, did not happen to real or wholly human people.

Land acknowledgments can undermine Indigenous sovereignty in ways that are both insidious and often incomprehensible to non-Indigenous people.

Land acknowledgments are not necessarily harmful if they are done in a way that is respectful of the Indigenous nations who claim the land, accurately tell the story of how the land passed from Indigenous to non-Indigenous control and chart a path forward for redressing the harm inflicted through the process of land dispossession. Along with a clear statement that the land needs to be restored to the Indigenous nation or nations that previously had sovereignty over the land by revealing a sincere commitment to respecting and enhancing Indigenous sovereignty.

This is not unrealistic: There are many creative ways to take restorative measures and even to give land back. If a land acknowledgment is discomforting and triggers uncomfortable conversations versus self-congratulation, it is likely on the right track.

There is more information regarding this from The Conversation link provided, edited and republished under a Creative Commons license:

Indigenous peoples are not relics of the past. Land acknowledgment is only one small part of supporting Indigenous communities. We hope to inspire others to stand in solidarity with Native nations by taking some or all the following support actions:

- Do your own research and homework on the Indigenous peoples, the history of the land and related treaties to whom it belongs.

- Use appropriate language and terms. Learn the pronunciation.

- Use past, present, and future tenses.

- Don't ask an Indigenous person to deliver a "welcome" statement for your organization.

- Build real, authentic relationships with Indigenous people.

- Compensate Indigenous people for their emotional labor.

- Understand displacement and how that plays into land acknowledgement.

- Donating time and money to Indigenous-led organizations.

- Amplify the voices of Indigenous people leading grassroots change movements.

- Return land and research ways to support returning land to Indigenous nations.

For my children Embry, Alana, & Rune.

CONTENTS

PREFACE

Dear Reader,

Dragonfly Saga is a creative body of works following my personal journey in life, revealing the infinite connections, or synchronicities, I have felt and perceived in a life of contemplation.

Part I embodies 'Tale of Dragonfly,' a five-book series that follows the titles and changes of the Daoist Five Seasons beginning with Late Summer and ending with the Return to Late Summer.

Tale of Dragonfly follows my own life inspired by, and in conjunction with, the myriad forms of esoteric and exoteric knowledge I have learned from, experienced, and perceived in this lifetime in communion with my own imagination and the stories of humanities interwoven past.

Part II of Dragonfly Saga is currently a beautifully chaotic web of inspiration, thought, idea, memory, and many other of the ten thousand things all being gathered into a wondrous sort of order; as is what follows Dragonfly Saga for this is one of those never-ending stories.

Dragonfly Saga's intention, one among many, is from a father to his children; more accurately, from an estranged father to his estranged children.

I have written Dragonfly Saga as a way for my children to know their father in a way that is not currently possible, due to the past actions and choices of myself, and the fears, shadows, and choices of others; none are to blame, yet all are held accountable, none more or less so than any other, myself included.

More importantly, perhaps, this work provides a focus for the questions my children may have and ask when the time comes that we are finally reunited, igniting wonderful conversations between us in truthfulness and transparency.

If life so happens in a way that we are never to see one another again in this lifetime, then perhaps this work will provide the only answer that truly matters, and I speak directly to you now, my children: I love you.

Embry, Alana, and Rune, as I write these words now, years have now passed since I have held you in my arms, since I have seen your faces or heard your voices and laughter; and still, I have no way of knowing just how long it will truly be until I do, or if I ever will again.

I miss listening to you, I miss talking to you, I miss being with you, and I miss simply watching you be yourselves.

There may be many things said about me, your father, but that I am a follower of rules will not be one of them. I can only hope you believe me and understand that it has been the most painful challenge of my life to attempt to follow these rules of not coming to you or speaking to you.

Some wounds are never meant to be healed in a single lifetime; and some scars never fade.

If you are reading this now, you may be wondering why I have chosen to tell stories as my way of speaking to you; perhaps you have remembered and already know; and perhaps you haven't thought about it at all and that time is yet to come.

Why do I tell these stories? I tell stories to help guide you to me. Whether they're stories I write and turn into books, or stories I tell from long ago with my voice, they are all for you. I tell stories because I love stories and because I love you. I tell them because when I am telling stories I feel connected to you; I remember when you were with me, reading to you, using my voice and voices, being every character, transporting us into the worlds of the story together; so when I tell these stories now, I am imagining I am telling them to you as you lay in your beds, or are cuddled beside me, looking at the pages as I read, or sitting in front of me, looking up at me, your eyes lit with imagination.

When I tell these stories I am with you in the past as I remember you, when I tell these stories I am with you now, wherever you are and may be, even though I cannot see you or speak to you; when I tell these stories I am with you in the future where we are reunited and together again; when I tell these stories the love I have and feel for you remains forever preserved, timeless, everlasting, and never-ending long after we have returned to being specks of star dust.

I tell stories to help you remember; I tell these stories to share my love for you with all. I tell these stories to play my part in helping us unite our shared past, present, future, waking, dreaming, life, death, and everything in between.

I tell stories to help me remember it all because it is beyond difficult to remember everyday that goes by without you beside me. Living life without each of you has been the greatest and most painful challenge of my lifetime, there is no more truer truth for me than this.

There are many other reasons why I tell stories, too, that are all very true; but this is the reason that is in and from my heart and soul. That reason is you, you are my heart.

I love you and I miss you, see you soon.

Love,

Dad

Shane Curtis Fike – https://linktr.ee/shanecurtisfike

"Run and find out. Grow your wings. Seek and find me. I am here, waiting." -Shane Curtis Fike

INTRODUCTION

"Hello there, Traveler. Yes, you, of course I see you, what an intriguing question. Would you like to hear a story?"

"You would, of course you would! Why else would you be here? Come, sit, and share this fire and brew with me."

"What's that? Where is here, how did you get here and where did these woods and this fire, and I, come from?"

"More curious questions, Traveler. How should I know how you got here? Where were you before? Were you at home, in a vehicle, a shop, a café? Was it night or was it day? Were you somewhere or nowhere, perhaps you were elsewhere? Were you sleeping, awake, or somewhere in between?"

"Is that so? Is that where you were?"

"And now you find yourself in this place you call here? From there to here in a dark wood with purple-gray swirling mists, rosy pink petals and leaves drifting and swirling like dervish through the gentle winds beneath a starry night sky; a sky filled with stars and constellations you do not recognize, of myriad colors and hues; standing before a mysterious hooded figure in all black, sitting before a mystical looking fire appearing to you to shimmer, shift, and dance with the very cadence and tone of my voice?"

"Quite right, Traveler, that is indeed strange.

As for where is here and where did these woods come from, another mystery, Traveler. They were here long before you got here and were already here when I arrived."

"Hmm? Oh, yes, clever! I suppose we could ask the trees. Do you speak Tree?"

"No? Unfortunate, then—another mystery left unsolved. Perhaps the answer will come in another time and another place.

Tell me Traveler, have you ever heard the tale of Dragonfly?"

"No, no, not the story of *the* dragonfly. This is not some half esoteric metaphor and half scientific method about the life cycles of that curious flying insectoid species of the family of Anisoptera of the order Odonata to be used as a self-inquiring comparison into your own inner psychology.

No, I would never presume to think you were in need, or seeking, such a thing. Besides that's been done to death, quite literally, to death, Traveler; most of the Freudians and Jungians and others who began such work are all quite literally dead.

No, I am referring to the mythical quest, the adventure, the story and tale, the saga of he who is named Dragonfly."

"What? Is he who is named Dragonfly also a dragonfly?

Well, of course Dragonfly is indeed a dragonfly, how ridiculous to be named Dragonfly but not be a dragonfly."

"Say again? Why is a dragonfly named Dragonfly?

Well, I suppose it's because during the time of this story things were named what they were. The sky was the sky and was named Sky, the moon was the moon and named Moon, the sun was the sun and named Sun; it was a simpler time, Traveler, things were a lot less confusing before things had names that were different from that which they were. Take your name for instance, Traveler—err, what is your name, by the way?"

"No, Traveler, your real name, that's a—oh, my apologies, that is your name.

Oh yes, that's a lovely name for a—erm, a…well, a—that is a lovely name, indeed, Traveler. A nod of congratulations to the decision-making capabilities of your progenitors. That is your name, then; but is your name what you are, Traveler?"

"No, I didn't think so."

"What's that? Is my name what I am? Of course, I told you, it keeps things simple."

"You have another question? By all means, Traveler, ask your questions, fire away. I am an open book, after all."

"Who am I? My apologies, Traveler, how rude of me. Nox Arcanum, humble storyteller, and guide at your service."

"Oh, that's a very clever question, Traveler. Were all dragonflies named Dragonfly? A very curious choice of tense as well. 'Were.' That would imply that you presume all dragonflies are no longer named Dragonfly, if ever they were all named Dragonfly, that they no longer all are.

A curious hypothesis you possess, Traveler. Perhaps we will find the answer to what you seek in the story, eh? Shall I tell it and you listen? Maybe we will transform your hypothesis into a full-blown theory together!"

"Where are we going? *Going?* We are *going* where we have already arrived, where we have never been, and where we never left—right here, right now, Traveler.

As you may have surmised, you have already wandered into a portal, gone through transmission, and emerged out of vision.

Don't be bashful, now, Traveler, you've come this far. Sit here, and listen to the stories told here of truth, of possibility, of thought and memory—and of wonder.

Hold this moment, here, take this breath and hear the tales of life and beyond, of original nature, of all within the all. Let the primordial fire enlighten the darkness surrounding you; be held and be comforted by it.

Watch, look, and see. Listen and feel; and be transported into a world—of transformation."

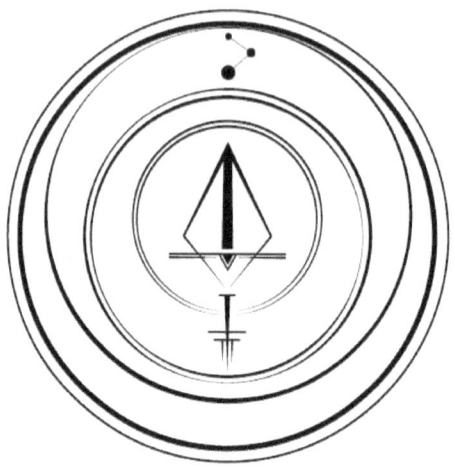

CHAPTER I

Butterfly and the Nymph

At the tail end of summer, in the between space of the season before autumn, where the temperature is beginning to descend, the presence of daylight is diminishing, and the leaves have only just begun their yellowing, where you can feel the change coming at any moment, a butterfly flaps its wings.

The butterfly has been journeying for quite a while and has grown weary; and so, she decides to land upon a rock to drink from the still waters of a lake.

She takes slow sips from the calm waters, looking across its reflective surface as she does and sees not her reflection, but two eyes wide and full of wonder, just beneath the surface, watching her, drifting slowly closer from the darkened depths of the glassy lake.

The butterfly flaps her wings in startled excitement, but immediately calms as those eyes make no movement in aggression; the eyes remind her of the same eyes, in color and curious shape, as her eldest son.

A smile and tear forms as she thinks of him and remembers how long it has been since she has seen him last, and she begins to wonder.

"Hello," says the curious-sounding creature as it breaches the surface, bobs up and down, and submerges again, blowing little bubbles as it does.

The Butterfly ponders to herself and makes a mental note to investigate, and reflect, on this first encounter later as she realizes she is unsure if the voice she is hearing is coming from within her memory of her son, or a coincidence; for they, the voice of memory, and the voice of now, sound much and almost the same in depth, cadence, melody, and tone.

"Hello," the butterfly says with a smile and sweet-sounding giggle.

"Who are you?" asks the creature, without a moment's hesitation or fear.

"I am Butterfly," she says, swelling with gratuitous pride for the chance to proclaim her revered name to another; "Who are you?" she asks.

The little creature makes a most unusual movement with those wonder-filled eyes, one that sends Butterfly's heart and wings aflutter, and yet another smile and tear form, caressing her cheeks.

The creature squints one eye, raises wide the other, simultaneously seeming skeptical, inquisitive, and a little mischievous; it slowly drifts just beneath the surface, blows a few bubbles, and gently breaches, returning its gaze normally to Butterfly.

"Hmmm, I do not know who I am," says the creature. "I do know what I am. I am *it.*"

Butterfly reveals her own skepticism at hearing the creature's self-proclamation.

"It?" she asks. "Are you sure you, are *it?*"

"No," says the creature, without skipping a beat, as if the question and the response were planned. "I am sure of nothing. I am curious."

Surely this creature knows and is sure of things, Butterfly thinks to herself. Questions form and rise in her mind in a flash and instant. She asks herself silently, *is it playing tricks and attempting to confuse me? Is it truly inquisitive and as innocent as it seems?*

She knows she could fly away and not be bothered with such questions and details; although, she is curious and remembers when she was once curious of the way of things, and their meanings. Butterfly makes her choice, in that instant, to stay and perhaps pass on what she has learned and what she believes she now knows.

She decides to ask questions of her own to see what this curious creature does know and is sure of.

"Interesting," says Butterfly. "Are you not sure of anything?"

"If I were sure," says the creature on cue; "then I could not learn anything new, for I would be sure I already knew it."

Butterfly is ready for the quick retort this time and has one of her own readily on the tip of her tongue.

"Aren't you sure the sun is shining in the day?" she asks. "And aren't you sure the moon is glowing at night?"

Butterfly expects a quick response in return but is instead met with a confused look and a pause as the creature descends, blows its bubbles from its little gills, and returns.

"What is the sun and the moon?" asks the creature.

All the memories of being beneath the sun flood Butterfly.

"The sun is what brings the morning dawn," she says with dearest reverence, "it is what gives the world light, warmth, and nourishment."

The creature smiles widely and gives a nod toward the midmorning sun as it nearly rises full out of the water in excitement.

"Oh, you mean Sister," it says. "The brilliant one."

Butterfly frowns in half pity and immediately dons her teacher's mantle.

"The sun cannot be your sister," she says. "It is not a living creature as you and me, but a giant ball of flame extremely far away that may never come nearer, or else we would all perish from its intense radiance and fire."

The creature's excited state immediately dissipates, and a look of sadness comes over it as it falls back into the water, nearly fully submerged.

"And the moon?" it asks in a quiet and mumbled whisper.

"The moon gives light within the darkness at night," says Butterfly, hoping her words will cheer the creature up, as they do her when she thinks of, and speaks, them aloud. "The moon raises and lowers the tides from its place in the sky and shows the passage of time by its phases."

Again, the creature perks up out of the water and nods toward the sky in the opposite direction of where the sun now sits.

"Oh, you mean Brother," it says. "The traveler."

Butterfly frowns yet again, pausing before speaking and allowing the frown to transform to a smile with care and ease.

"The moon cannot be your brother," she says. "It is not a living creature as you and me but a dusty rock floating beside the Earth that reflects the light of the sun."

The creature closes its eyes and twists itself toward the sun, then to the other side as if straining to hear something off in the distance; it descends beneath the surface, blows its bubbles, and comes back; and it opens its eyes, gazing upon Butterfly.

"What is the Earth?" it asks.

Butterfly laughs out loud with genuine surprise and glee at the awareness this creature is, indeed, not attempting to trick and confuse her; but is genuinely curious of the ways of the world.

"You are curious," she says with a joyous smile.

"Yes," says the creature, with a singular nod in full agreement.

Butterfly surveys the land around them, thinking of a simple and direct answer of what she knows the Earth to be.

"The Earth is all around us," she says; "it is the land, the waters, the air; all of life lives and dies upon it. All that you see is of the Earth."

The creature repeats its skeptical, yet inquisitive, eye maneuver again.

"Oh, you mean Mother," it says.

The firm directness of its tone implies to Butterfly that the creature is not asking but telling; and she finds herself mirroring the same eye expression, though it is her own version, and does not mirror that of the creature, or her son's from memory; though, the intent and meaning are there, and the resemblance may be seen—and witnessed—if you know where to look.

Butterfly feels more than one fluttering, a small amount of pity for this creature not knowing what she knows; and something more is there, deeper, that she will have to investigate later, she decides, instead of speaking on such curious things in this moment.

"The Earth cannot be your mother," she says. "It is not a living creature as you and me, but made of dirt, rock, plant, water, and sky."

Butterfly watches for what the creature's reaction will be to this new realization and sees the telltale sign of deep sadness; but with a quick recovery and a question already formulated.

"What is sky?" asks the creature.

"The sky is what is up above," says Butterfly, quickly, with all reverence for what she believes the sky to truly be; with a daring hope of deterring any more sadness from the creature. "The spaciousness all around you from the ground all the way up, and out, among the stars is the sky."

The creature nods its head and closes its eyes in a blink, giving a few more nods, as if reaffirming something to itself.

"Oh, you mean Father," it says.

Butterfly feels the desired requirement to clear up this creature's confusions as quickly and completely as possible.

"The sky cannot be your father," she says. "It is not a living creature as you and me; it is only air."

The creature does not take its eyes from Butterfly's gaze as it descends beneath the surface, blows out its bubbles, and returns with yet another question.

"What is air?" it asks.

An easy enough answer for a simple question, Butterfly thinks to herself, with a smile.

"The air is what you breathe in and blow out," she says; "that fills the spaces from ground to cloud, and above, until you reach the outer places."

The look of mischief and skeptical inquisitiveness returns, and the creature turns its head to the side, with what Butterfly can only describe as a cheeky smirk.

"I'm a nymph," says the creature. "I breathe water, not this air."

Butterfly flaps her wings once with a sharp snap in agitation, immediately catching herself with a laugh, her kind demeanor instantly returning.

"You breathe the air that is in the water," she says.

The nymph does not release its look of skeptical inquisitiveness; indeed, it seems to have grown, if such a thing is possible; and it nods its head as it sinks beneath the surface.

It stays there for quite a few repetitions of tiny bubbles, and as Butterfly watches it contemplating through the subtle bursts of breakthrough, she reflects again on just how much this creature reminds her of her son.

A formed tear begins its slow descent down her cheek, the drop hits the water and sends out a wave of ripples across the lake, and she silently watches until the waters become still again; she notices the nymph has already returned to the surface and is staring at her, and it appears to notice that her attention has returned to the present.

"You have taught me many new things I did not know before," says the nymph. "Lovely names and titles, thank you; though, now I am sad. Where before I had a brother, sister, mother, and father; now I only have un-living things surrounding me, and more questions." The nymph pauses for half a heartbeat. "Who taught you these things?" it asks.

Butterfly sucks in her breath and flutters her wings at hearing this question, her mind toils into overthinking overload as her own questions of how to respond race through her thoughts: *How could she, and how would she explain where she had learned of these things; of whom it was that told her of everything she knows, is, and believes; of the majesty and the reverence she holds most dear? The importance of such a description. How would she say it?* And as she asks the questions in her mind, she receives the answer.

"The voice carried on a breeze," she says, smiling in gratitude as she speaks the words she was gifted, with all the sacrality she feels and can muster.

"What is a breeze?" asks the nymph, with seeming indifference to her reverence.

Containing her mixed feelings of disappointment for the nymph not feeling what she was putting forth in her simple words, with a laughter and appreciation that, of course, this one would just have another question; Butterfly begins to formulate a beautifully detailed description of what a breeze is in her mind.

"It is the wind—"

"Oh, the Wind! I know the Wind," shouts the nymph, completely shocking her out of her own deep revery, the nymph excitedly begins jumping up and down from the surface, nearly floating upon the very air they now speak of. "We have great fun, the Wind and me. The Wind makes waves on the water's surface I play in and use to escape from the big fish that want to eat me, we have races, and we talk just as you and I are right now."

Finding herself just as excited at the nymph's description of its love of the Wind, she flaps her wings along with its jumps, hoots, and hollers until the nymph's voice, words, and elation fade away into still silence.

A look of near despair falls over the nymph as it slowly descends beneath the surface to blow its bubbles for a passing moment; and Butterfly patiently waits until the nymph breaches the calm waters once again.

"What is wrong?" asks Butterfly.

"I am confused," says the nymph, looking at Butterfly and matching her gaze in sincerity. "It was the Wind who taught me about Brother, Sister, Mother, and Father; how to talk to them, and about everything and nothing. Why would the Wind teach me one thing and you another?"

Butterfly believes she knows the answer to this question; but also knows it would take some thinking to formulate the necessary words of conveyance properly, she would have to wait and listen for the proper way to provide such instruction.

"Curious," she says, in what she hopes to be a consoling way to return the conversation to a more uplifting tone for the nymph. "I will ponder this."

Much to her surprise, her words have an adverse effect on the nymph, and while he wears his expression of mischievousness, skepticism, and inquisitiveness, it much more resembles a look of now determination and commitment.

"While you ponder, I'm going to ask the Wind," proclaims the nymph.

"How will you speak to the Wind from under the water?" asks Butterfly, shocked and taken aback by the nymph's assuredness.

Hurriedly, but not panicked, the nymph begins looking around left to right, right to left; after a moment of this, the nymph begins gliding through the water toward the shore, apparently finding what it is seeking.

Butterfly, excited and intrigued, flutters after and alongside the nymph, mere inches above the surface of the water.

"I won't," says the nymph, without taking its gaze from the unknown destination. "I will emerge."

"Emerge?" asks Butterfly, even more entranced and finding herself now curiously intrigued.

The nymph reaches the shore where tall grass and reeds rise from the waters as Butterfly lands upon one of the nearby reed stalks; and she watches the nymph as it darts from one to another, quick as a firefly's blink.

"Yes," says the nymph, without turning its gaze toward Butterfly. "I will leave these waters I have called home for years behind, I will find a strong blade of grass or reed, and I will grow my wings; then I will fly with the Wind, and we will speak, and I will ask questions."

Disappointment creeps upon Butterfly; she had momentary hope that something was about to happen now; instead, in this moment, she feels sad and compelled to relay the news that such a thing would take a very long time.

"I have done this," she says; "but it takes so awfully long to go through the transformation and metamorphosis—near a month, or more, for me to go from crawling Caterpillar to fluttering Butterfly."

The nymph does not falter or even seem shocked or abashed at the hearing and telling of what Butterfly had believed would be debilitating news.

In fact, the nymph seems to have found a chosen reed; and as he descends beneath the surface for a final time, he lets out a long stream of bubbles, longer than any of the times before; and then breaches the surface, without looking back, and begins to climb the reed stalk.

Butterfly flutters closer and lands on another reed beside the one the nymph has chosen.

"Another question, then, for the Wind," says the nymph, as it swiftly climbs. "Why does is take you a month to do what I can do in a few hours?"

Butterfly is taken aback in full; *surely this could not be possible,* she wonders to herself.

"A few hours?" she asks. "You mean to say you will change your body, and sprout two wings from your back in just a few hours?"

The nymph seems to scoff in its determination, unwilling to be distracted or deterred from its purpose.

"No," says the nymph, in a near-mocking tone. "Of course not, how ridiculous, I will have four wings."

Butterfly shakes her head, held in true amazement, as she looks at the nymph, watching him climb the reed, thinking to herself on how this creature has instantaneously gone from childlike innocence—full of questions and claiming to know nothing—to now, it seems as if it were the teacher; and something else, something that once again reminds her of her eldest son. He was a warrior too.

"Truly?" asks Butterfly, whispering both to herself and to the nymph.

The nymph laughs and does what Butterfly can only describe as a cheeky smirk, then the creature becomes completely still, closing its eyes.

"Watch this," says the nymph from within that smirkiest grin.

The day continues and passes as the sun moves along its predetermined path across the sky. Butterfly watches in silence, ruminating on her conversation with the creature, this nymph, growing ever more curious of what questions may be asked, what new and unknown things may be learned; and she waits, watching as the nymph's body hardens in its stillness; asking herself, *is that movement coming from inside?*

The daytime becomes twilight, and in these hours the body of the nymph cracks and splits.

A creature with those overlarge, wondrous, beautiful eyes truly does emerge from the encasement. It has a long, thin tail protruding from its body, and just as the nymph said, there are one, two, three, and four wings.

Butterfly sucks in her breath and waits for the creature to speak, a little afraid of what the transformation might have done, it cannot be understated that this new form is quite intimidating to the delicate Butterfly; she holds her faith and trust, and silently waits.

More time passes, and as it does, something magical is happening before her eyes; the four wings, and the body itself, of this creature become iridescent; beautifully glimmering, shimmering, and shining with colors of green, blue, indigo, and purple upon its wings radiating the full spectrum of the rainbow, the beauty and magnificence cannot be denied.

Butterfly finds herself smiling and unable to contain her silence any longer as the creature lifts from the reed and begins flying loops, quick as lightning spins, and dazzling dashes across the sky—the nymph seems to dance and race the very wind, as it had described.

"Remarkable, magnificent, and wonderful!" Butterfly shouts up to the creature. "How is this possible?" she asks.

The creature turns, dips, and dives directly in front of Butterfly, and smiles; and there they all are, those familiar things: that mischievous, skeptical inquisitiveness, that cheeky smirk, and that all-too-familiar voice.

"It is what I do," says the creature. "I am Dragonfly."

CHAPTER II

Grandfather and the Two Brothers

Newly emerged from his transformation, Dragonfly continues to dip, dive, and dash in grand designs and patterns all around Butterfly as she watches in glee and amazement.

"Are you with the Wind, Dragonfly?" asks Butterfly, reaching for him with her shouting voice.

Dragonfly immediately stops and hovers a reed's length above where Butterfly remains perched, he turns to the left and pauses, and then to the right and pauses.

"No and nay," he says. "The Wind is not here!"

Butterfly feels a sense of dread for a moment at the thought of there being no Wind, but then she looks at Dragonfly up there floating and hovering in the air, and she smiles and begins fluttering up to greet him.

"Are you sure?" she asks, watching as Dragonfly sways back and forth for a moment.

"There is wind, wisps, and air," says Dragonfly; "but the Wind? The Wind is not here now."

"How can that be so?" asks Butterfly.

"Another question to add to the list," says Dragonfly as he looks onward.

Butterfly flattens her wings and glides back and forth, matching Dragonfly's sway in the air.

"How do you find the Wind?" she asks.

Dragonfly remains silent, and three times he sways back and forth.

"I have never had to find the Wind," he says. "It has always just been there when I wasn't looking, and it always seemed to find me. This will be a first, for me, to go seeking the Wind."

Butterfly dips up and down as she continues to glide back and forth in understanding of Dragonfly's meaning.

"Perhaps that is how we find the Wind," she says; "we don't look, we go; and the Wind will find us."

Again, Dragonfly pauses with another three turns back and forth in his sway.

"I can think of no argument to this plan," he says. "I say, yay."

"Hurray!" shouts Butterfly with a victorious fluttering flap of her wings. "Then to which way?"

Dragonfly looks down at the waters of the lake that has been his house and home for many years, and as quickly as he is able, he descends and dives directly for the surface before circling and spinning just above it, splashing the water, and sending waves of ripples out across the mirror-glass lake from the point of his reflection.

With another spin, he shoots straight up into the air and arrives beside Butterfly, looking toward the horizon.

"I would like to go to the forest," says Dragonfly. "I have never been."

"I adore the forest," says Butterfly as she immediately begins to flutter and fly in the direction of the wooded forest stretched out before them. "To the forest it is."

Into the forest Butterfly and Dragonfly go. Butterfly fluttering along at her pace with Dragonfly zipping here and there and back again, never straying too far from Butterfly. Always can she see him. She smiles as Dragonfly explores every nook and cranny of this new world that he is discovering for the first time.

Butterfly floats just above the highest of the tall grass and flowers that make up the forest floor as Dragonfly ascends, spins, darts, and dashes up among the trees and their branches; his iridescent scales glimmering off the rays of sun that shine through the leaves here and there, while Butterfly's golden wings shine in contrast to the green, combining with the beauty of the many flowering blooms that she stops to rest and drink from now and again.

She watches as Dragonfly inspects the entirety of this forested world he is immersed in; she watches as he hovers, transfixed, over a knot in the side of a large oak tree.

"I did not know trees had eyes," says Dragonfly.

Butterfly looks again at the knot in the tree's trunk and looks around at all the other trees with their knots and suddenly feels a thousand eyes upon her.

"Yes," she says; "they can be quite frightening at times."

"Frightening?" asks Dragonfly, cocking his head to one side. "Hmm. I suppose it could be frightening to be seen by eyes that never close but always see."

Dragonfly turns and dives toward Butterfly and hovers before her, leaning close.

"Lucky for me," he says in a whisper, with a wink and smirk, as if he does not want the trees to hear his words; "I like to be seen."

Butterfly laughs, and Dragonfly spins upward into a ray of sunlight shining from the trees' leaves to the forest floor below, and his glimmering scales send out their own rays of emanating colorful light in all directions. They both laugh as they continue their exploration through the forest.

After traveling for nearly an entire cycle of the sun's path across the sky from east to west, Butterfly and Dragonfly begin to grow tired. Even Dragonfly's quick movements are slowed to stillness as he travels at the same pace in steady rhythm beside Butterfly.

They come upon a row of many flowers atop a small hill with a boulder in the center, creating a multicolored ring of flora around it. The flowers are beautiful, and as Dragonfly and Butterfly come in for a closer look, they notice there are sharp thorns attached to the stems of the flowers; and woven between the forest floor and the blooms is hidden an entire labyrinth of thorny vines; indeed, the entire floor surrounding the boulder is one large briar patch, completely hidden by the large blooms of colorful flowers.

Dragonfly and Butterfly, nearly mesmerized by the scene, come to rest upon two of the flowers near the boulder; and as the hush of silence comes from the stillness of their insect wings, they become aware of a new sound. The sound of rushing water.

"What is that?" asks Dragonfly.

"Water," says Butterfly. "Have we circled back to your lake?" she asks.

"No," responds Dragonfly. "That is not the still lake; it is moving water."

"Moving water," says a new and unknown voice, breaking through the silence with a short chuckle, startling Dragonfly and Butterfly enough to rise and hover over the flowers they are resting upon. "I like that," says the stranger.

Dragonfly and Butterfly turn together; and there, upon the large boulder—that they were sure was vacant when they arrived—lounges a fox, appearing ancient and lying in a sphinxlike position, as if he had always been there. A most curious riddle.

"Who are you?" asks Dragonfly as he drifts and settles back onto the flower. "How did you get there?"

"Beautiful questions, Dragonfly," says the ancient fox with a laugh. "Don't you know my name?"

Dragonfly pauses as Butterfly now settles back on her own flower and listens. She too is curious how the old fox has managed to get atop the boulder when all the ground is covered in thorns. She watches another moment pass as Dragonfly looks up at the ancient fox, and the fox stares right back at him, unblinking.

"Grandfather," Dragonfly finally whispers.

"A simple form of the forest, with a function," says the old fox, chuckling with a familiar smirk that reminds Butterfly of Dragonfly's own.

Butterfly also remembers words she heard long ago.

"Beware the foxes," she says, finding herself unable to stop from saying them aloud.

"Well, I can't disagree now can I, little Butterfly?" asks Grandfather Fox, tilting his head and laughing softly. "Beware. Be aware, indeed. Clever and swift are we. Did you know that there is a butterfly in a land far from here that carries a poison strong enough to kill six cats?"

Butterfly flutters her wings and opens her maw to respond.

"What's a cat?" asks Dragonfly, before Butterfly can speak, and she flaps her wings with a tick and snap of anxiousness, as Grandfather Fox continues his gentle laughter of amusement.

"Another beautiful question, Dragonfly," says Grandfather Fox. "A cat is a cousin of mine, also swift and clever, in between things and masters of stillness and travel. They, too, carry the mark of the trickster. Be aware when listening to cats. You will earn what you get by following their advice and lead."

"The same can be said for you, Grandfather Fox," says Butterfly, refusing to miss her chance to speak her mind.

"You are not wrong," says Grandfather Fox, turning his gaze directly to Butterfly with a smirk and nod.

"Grandfather, what is that moving water we hear?" asks Dragonfly, oblivious to the banter and unspoken unease emitting from Butterfly toward Grandfather Fox. "Where is the sound coming from?"

"Fly above the treetops, Dragonfly," says Grandfather Fox, nodding upward, cranking his neck, and pointing his snout straight up. "Keep your back to the setting sun and look outward to the east, where the sun will rise again; and then come back and tell me what you have seen."

Without hesitating, Dragonfly soars up to and through the branches, zigging and zagging until he's out of sight and not even the gentle thundering of his wings can be heard. Grandfather Fox chuckles as he watches him go upward, out of sight, and looks down at Butterfly.

"He is quick, fast, swift, and clever, that one," says Grandfather Fox. "It will be difficult for you to keep up with him on this journey; he will learn stillness and spacious pacing from you. And you, from him, will learn quickening and contemplation. Be aware, Butterfly. There will be fear but be not afraid. Perhaps, together, you will find the true balance."

Butterfly wants to react immediately; thoughts begin racing through her mind at the words the old fox has spoken to her—thoughts of so many things. She begins to attempt to formulate a response when, instead, she finds an unexpected question.

"How can I trust you?" she asks.

"The sun soon sets," Grandfather Fox says with a nod to the flowers. "Rest and sleep here among the blooms, guarded by the thorns where none may reach you in slumber. I will keep watch, and when—and if—you awaken in the morning, perhaps then you will trust me. Before then, all you can do is choose to believe me or not. It is your choice, Butterfly."

Butterfly listens and begins to think when the sound of Dragonfly's winged thundering interrupts the silence as he returns, spinning and landing atop the large flower bloom, sending it swaying back and forth for a few moments.

"Snakes!" shouts Dragonfly in an entirely excited state. "Grandfather, there are two huge serpents shining and glimmering as they slither and cut through the forest and the entire land for as far as the eye can see. They are twisting into one another! Two becomes one, and then they split again, intertwining, and coming together here and there. It is their hissing we hear!"

Butterfly feels terror in her heart. *Two gigantic serpents so near?* she asks herself. *What place have we come to?* she begins to wonder as she feels the fear rising in her, overtaking her.

"Snakes, you say!" says Grandfather Fox with a booming laughter straight from his belly. "Oh, Dragonfly, those are not serpents; those are wolves."

"Wolves?" asks Dragonfly, cocking his head as he looks back up at the treetops and then returns his gaze to Grandfather Fox.

"That is a river, boy," says Grandfather Fox as he resumes his gentle and quiet demeanor, chuckling and shaking his head. "A single river by name of the Two Wolf Brothers River."

"Where does the river go?" Dragonfly asks, without hesitating.

"Where all rivers go," says Grandfather Fox softly, looking in the direction of where the river can be heard coming from. "To see what may be seen; and that is where you will find the Wind."

"How do you know we are looking for the Wind?" asks Butterfly, fluttering her wings.

Without breaking his gaze, Grandfather Fox responds still softly, "The Wind told me."

"You know the Wind?" asks Dragonfly, excitedly.

"Of course I know the Wind, boy," says Grandfather Fox, his eyes on Dragonfly. "How do you think I may be so swift as to take the fish from the bear as the bear takes the fish from the river?"

"Grandfather, why is it called the Two Wolf Brothers River?" asks Dragonfly while nodding in acceptance and understanding.

"Ah, now that is a good story," says Grandfather Fox, taking a deep breath and returning the nod with one of his own and a chuckle. "I shall tell it to you as the last light of the sun dips beneath the horizon. Here you will rest, and tomorrow follow the river; stay upon and near it, keep going, and you will find the Wind."

Grandfather Fox looks up toward the tree, the rays of light shining through their leaves, the illuminations dissipating as the sun begins to set, night begins to rise, and with it, the moon.

The eyes of Grandfather Fox shimmer and gleam with the same iridescence of Dragonfly's scales.

"Where the two rivers come together and become one is where the story both begins and ends," says Grandfather Fox, lowering his voice with a tone that seems to echo through the trees of the forest as he pauses for a moment and looks at first Butterfly, then Dragonfly, and lastly toward the direction of the very river he is speaking of.

"The two rivers are the two wolf brothers. Both come from down the mountains and through the valley, traveling to their destination. Both believe they can get there faster and with clearer waters than the other; and so, they clash.

Here, at this very spot, is the first place they come together.

One wolf brother is what has come to be known as the word 'evil.' That brother's river is filled with all manner of anger, envy, jealousy, sorrow, regret, greed, arrogance, self-pity, guilt, resentment, inferiority, lies, false pride, superiority, and illusion; and its name is Ego.

The other wolf brother is what has come to be known as the word 'good.' That brother's river is filled with all manner of joy, peace, love, hope, serenity, humility, kindness, benevolence, generosity, empathy, truth, and compassion; and its name is Faith.

Both rivers have their spaces of stillness and calm, both have their white waters and rapids, both have deep, dark pools, both have cascading falls, both have predators and prey, and both lead to the same destination, each clashing with the other to arrive there first."

"Grandfather, if they both get to the same place, does it matter which river you take?" asks Dragonfly, unable to prevent himself from interrupting.

"Of course, it matters," says Grandfather Fox, speaking slowly and not removing his fixed gaze from the direction of the river.

"How do we know which river is which?" asks Butterfly, feeling curious herself; "Which is the good river called Faith, and which is the evil river called Ego?"

"You cannot know that until you are upon the river," Grandfather Fox responds in the same slow cadence, never removing his eyes from the direction of the river.

A moment of silence passes between the three. Dragonfly and Butterfly are unsure if Grandfather Fox has finished the story or if he is waiting to continue.

"Grandfather, do you know which river is which?" asks Dragonfly.

"Yes," says Grandfather Fox, turning his eyes to Dragonfly.

"Have you been to the rivers' destination?" asks Dragonfly.

"Yes," says Grandfather Fox, maintaining his unblinking gaze upon Dragonfly.

"Which river gets there first?" Dragonfly asks, wondering if he has been the one leading up to this question or if he has been being led up to asking it.

A sly grin spreads across Grandfather Fox's face with a smirk, and his eyes gleam as moonlit rays now descend through the trees and the forest becomes aglow, awash, and bathed in a bluish light of the full moon glimmering off the sharp teeth of Grandfather Fox.

"The one that gets fed the most." * replies Grandfather Fox with a heartfelt, gentle chuckle.

Butterfly hears this and feels a strange sensation of both unease and calm move through her. She looks to Dragonfly, expecting him to keep asking questions; and when she looks at him, she sees a complete stillness has come over him, and she realizes she cannot even tell if he is breathing; he appears as but a statue.

She finds the excitement and adventure this day has taken over and become has brought her to complete exhaustion, and she can no longer think. She looks from Dragonfly to Grandfather Fox and notices that she feels very vulnerable and afraid, but too weakened and overcome with exhaustion to do anything about it.

"Be not afraid," says Grandfather Fox. "I will watch over you as you sleep in this place."

Butterfly feels the embrace of sleep beginning to take her, and she stops resisting, allowing herself to completely succumb to slumbers invitation; as she looks down at the flower she has been resting upon, curiosity pervades her drowsiness.

"Grandfather, what is the name of these flowers that grow here?" asks Butterfly through a wide-mouthed yawn.

"Does it matter the name?" asks Grandfather Fox, his voice cutting through the fog of sleep taking Butterfly to the realm of dream. "Would the flower still not smell as sweet or be as beautiful if it were known by any other name?"

"I was just curious if they had a name," says Butterfly as her eyes close and she sees nothing but comforting darkness, sleep fully embracing her save a final moment of wakefulness and presence.

"Well in that case," says Grandfather Fox, smiling, seeing Butterfly has drifted into the dream world and knowing his words will reach her in that place between sleep and awake. "They are named..."

The ancient fox's words drift along into the nothingness and the ether of Butterfly's dreamscapes as sleep takes her fully.

Butterfly opens her eyes, slowly at first, not entirely aware of herself or remembering anything. All at once she remembers it in entirety. She shoots up with worry and fright; and not knowing whether to expect danger or not, she looks around frantically for any sign of Grandfather Fox or Dragonfly.

She looks to the boulder where Grandfather Fox had been lounging. It now stands empty. She looks to the flower next to her where Dragonfly had been, though not really looking at it as she doesn't fully believe he will be there. Already she is thinking and turning to where she will look next; but there he is, Dragonfly, sitting still and watching her with a curious look on his face, and he is smirking. She cannot be sure why, but this time, that smirk agitates her.

"You thought he was going to eat us, didn't you?" asks Dragonfly with a gentle laugh, the light tone of his voice breaking through her agitation before it can erupt into anger.

"It's not funny," says Butterfly with a frown, the panic and fear settling within her.

"It's a little funny if you think about it," says Dragonfly with a shrug as he turns and looks toward where the sound of the river is emanating, the jovial laughter in his voice dissipating.

"Did you speak with Grandfather Fox further after I took my slumber?" asks Butterfly.

"We spoke more, but I, too, was drifting," says Dragonfly, hovering above the flower and facing the direction of the river; "and it is difficult to know what was said here and what was spoken in dream."

"Do you remember anything from your talk?" asks Butterfly, curious what Dragonfly and Grandfather Fox spoke on, but understanding the great challenge of remembering things from when one is falling into the mysterious realm of dream.

"I remember he told us how we may find the Wind, and I remember his answer to your question of the name of these flowers," says Dragonfly, continuing to hover above the flower.

Butterfly perks up at this. That memory escaped her, and now it has come rushing back, and she can feel a sense that she heard and knows the name of the flowers, but she cannot grasp it or remember; and she tries so desperately to think and force the name to materialize in her mind.

"Would you like me to tell you?" asks Dragonfly.

Butterfly almost blurts out in affirmation that yes, indeed, she wants to know, but then she hesitates and thinks on it.

"Tell me when I need something to remind me to smile," she says.

"As you wish," Dragonfly says with a gentle laugh and affirming nod.

"To the two rivers, then?" asks Butterfly, fluttering her wings, joining Dragonfly in the air, and flying toward the sound of moving water as Dragonfly begins his darting and dashing dance, echoing her enthusiasm.

"Yes," he says. "To the river."

CHAPTER III – PART 1

Grandmother and the Weaving

Dragonfly and Butterfly have been traveling for an entire expanse of the sun rising from the east to near now setting in the west, seeking the Wind to ask their questions, following the river as Grandfather Fox had suggested, with Dragonfly feasting and darting playfully while Butterfly stops, now and then, to enjoy the nectar of the luscious flowers.

The day begins to darken into night; and a drip, and drop, from the sky foretells the coming of rain. Dragonfly and Butterfly see a small cave off the river's bank where they might make refuge from the night and its perils.

"Not too far in," Butterfly says with a cautious tone in her voice.

But Dragonfly's curiosity and swiftness gets the better of him, and further in he goes to the darkness of the cave's unknowns.

"We don't know what could be waiting in the dark," continues Butterfly, reluctantly following Dragonfly deeper into the cave with a heavy sigh and exaggerated rolling of her eyes.

"Exactly," says Dragonfly; "and I wonder what it is."

"Hopefully, nothing," says Butterfly.

"Nothing would still be something," says Dragonfly.

Butterfly glances back toward the entrance of the cave as the last light of the sun dips below the horizon, enveloping the cave in pitch blackness.

She turns back to call out to Dragonfly when she finds herself held in silence, a still silence as complete as the cave is dark and black. There is no sound.

What is missing? she wonders. *What was there before that is not there now? What is gone for there to be such total silence?*

Then she remembers, and she knows; it is the humming of Dragonfly's wings that is no longer present, and fear grips her fluttering butterfly heart.

"Butterfly, stop!" Dragonfly's voice calls out, nearer than expected. "No! Go back!" Dragonfly continues to shout in a panic.

Butterfly finds herself not only held in silence but in stillness. There is no force or object that seems to stop her movement, though stopped in totality has it been. Her wings do not flap or flutter; she cannot bend, twist, or turn; she is held in full stillness, unable to see or hear anything but complete, formless black; without sound, save that of her ever-loudening beating heart, filling with fear.

Butterfly forces all of her will to give her the courage to speak aloud.

"Dragonfly, what is this?" she asks, the volume of her words a stammering whisper being all that she may dare. "Where are we?"

"We are caught in a web," says Dragonfly. "Do not speak or move. Hold and let me think and feel."

Butterfly realizes just how close Dragonfly is as he speaks; noticing they are nearly touching as his scent fills her frightened senses. With that awareness, shapes begin to form before Butterfly's eyes, she can see the shimmering and gleaming of Dragonfly's wings and scales, his iridescence taking form, though the coloring is different.

A strangely colored light begins to glow throughout the cave radiating from unknown sources; first a dark blue in the black, then whitening to a lavender purple, emanating from the now revealed fungi throughout the cave's floor, walls, and ceiling.

The violet glowing exposes the truth of their placement and predicament. Before them, all around them, encompassing them, is the most intricate webbing ever seen or witnessed, thick and solid as a fog below and connected to the floor of the cave, filled with bones and carcasses of the long dead.

The webbing and weaving begin to discern patterns as it rises above to the ceiling of the cave—intricate and spiraling, telling a story of beginning to end, and beginning again, and again, and again. Curves, circles, lines, shapes, and patterns shine like crystal strands with that lavender hue.

Even higher there are crisscrossing threads and lines going from here to there, cocoons holding those barely living in suspension; shells and carcasses of the freshly dead, gently spinning on the ends of their threads, still clinging by their death grip.

Nestled in floating webbing, here and there, are cloud-like orbs seeming to hum and throb. Egg sacs, new life to bring new death and continue the cycle.

"Butterfly, is any part of you free?" asks Dragonfly, whispering with excitement in his voice.

For the first time, now that the cave is illuminated enough to see, Butterfly takes inventory of herself. She begins gently stretching her limbs to see where there may yet be movement, extending her wings, circling her body and head, attempting to find what yet may be moved through her. There. She found it; her two forelegs may stretch and extend out before her.

"Yes," she says, the tremble of fear in her voice now lined with a gentle hopefulness. "I can reach out my forelegs."

"Can you reach my wings?" asks Dragonfly. "They are free on this side, if you can but free one other, I will break us out and free us from this entrapment."

Butterfly surveys Dragonfly's wings where they are stuck to the webbing. His upper wing closest to her is held only by a single strand of the web.

"I can," she says as she reaches out to grab hold but hesitates. "How am I to free it?" she asks, the hope in her voice beginning to lose its grip. "Won't I become stuck as soon as I touch it?"

"Very carefully," says Dragonfly. "Slowly and quietly, with tender force, focus and keep going."

Butterfly reaches out and hesitates again, afraid she will become even more entrapped in the webbing.

"Trust me," says Dragonfly, whispering ever softly, as if he hears and feels her very thoughts.

Butterfly reaches out slowly and begins to tenderly scratch and pull at the thread of webbing, the lightest and softest feathering of a touch and tug hovering so delicately between the tip of her limb and the thread; no living eye could witness the microcosmic touch of space in between the two.

Slowly, Butterfly notices the thread is layered, and the layers begin to unfold. The hope in her heart is renewed and she continues with eagerness.

"Slowly," says Dragonfly, his whisper of caution calling out to steady her hand.

Butterfly stops and calms herself by taking a breath and beginning again, slowly, and deliberately. As she continues, she notices the vibrations moving through the layers of the webbing's thread, and a gleam catches her notice from the corner of her eye.

Before she can remark on the subtle vibrations of the thread to Dragonfly, terror and dread overwhelm her, and she stops pulling at the thread, frozen and held in fear.

The gleam in the cave is a nestled cluster, much like the sacs of eggs, which can be seen, as can the reality of their predicament; although, this cluster is not white and throbbing of fluffed webbing, these orbs are black and shining.

The orbs are not simply something that is there; they are some things that are looking and seeing; there are eight of them, shining violet with white upon black, and they are looking at, and seeing, Butterfly. The orbs begin to move, upward and toward; and so, too, does the body of that which they are attached—the body and those eyes of the spider.

"Keep going, Butterfly," says Dragonfly, his whisper dispelling her from the terror she is held within by the giant spider's gaze.

"Butterfly?" asks a crone's voice, ancient, and echoing throughout the cavern as a hushed whisper, fully encompassed with a bass and tremor that is much more felt in the body than it is heard in the mind. "Butterfly," continues the crone-voice; "It has been many an age since there has been a butterfly in my weaving."

The spider continues to raise from the lower lair of its webbing and extends its unfolding limbs toward the two stuck in her web.

"Many moths, yes, attracted to the soft glow of the fungi," says the old spider. "But a true butterfly? Not since the elders came from high. The colors will be a wondrous monument to my weaving."

Butterfly's heart flutters furiously, and she continues steadily plucking at the single thread of web as the old, and enormous, spider approaches closer.

"And a most beautiful weaving it is, Grandmother Spider," says Dragonfly, his words nearly stopping Butterfly's beating heart. "A tapestry that tells the tale of the all, it is, I see."

Grandmother Spider pauses for a moment and then continues slowly toward them.

"Clever one," she says. "You see much with your flattery." Grandmother Spider stops again, shifting all eight of her eyes to Dragonfly. "And what are you, shiny thing, something new?"

Dragonfly does not hesitate in his response, and Butterfly is reminded of their first meeting when he was but a nymph in the water.

"A little new, quite old, and in between. I am Dragonfly," says Dragonfly, the lack of any hesitation in his response bringing an image to Butterfly's mind of their first meeting and conversation when he was but a nymph in the water; and his very words inciting an image of him bowing his head; and she imagines that is exactly what he would be doing if he were able to move his body that was still stuck fast in the web, the very web that he is now praising; and that she is desperately attempting to breakthrough without fainting in fear or revealing herself to the many eyes of the spider he is naming Grandmother.

"Indeed, you are," says Grandmother Spider in her crone voice. "Dragonfly, look how you shine, so many delicious colors of light—an entire spectrum."

Grandmother Spider is now a mere step from them, the threads of web vibrating as the spider comes closer.

"You should see my shine in the light, Grandmother," says Dragonfly. "Let us go out into the moonlight and I shall show you the glimmering."

Grandmother Spider cackles gently, her face and maw a mere gnat's breath distance from Dragonfly's large eyes.

"Clever, Dragonfly," she says. "I think not."

"Pity, Grandmother, you are missing a most magnificent sight," says Dragonfly, eliciting another image in Butterfly's mind of his telltale raising of one eye and lowering the other in quizzical expression; though she dares not remove her eyes from her work on the delicate strand of webbing to confirm her vision.

"Grandmother, what is that in the back of your cave?" asks Dragonfly, seeming unperturbed that Grandmother Spider will not release them from the webbing, and nodding his head—as much as he is able—to the far end of the cave.

Grandmother Spider cackles again, this time with even more glee, as she turns slowly in the direction of the cave's end; and for the first time, Butterfly sees an overlarge stone basin filled with seeds and surrounded by fungi and moss of many different colors. A single drop of water every so often drips from the ceiling of the cave into the stone basin of seeds.

"That, Dragonfly, is the cauldron of the seeds of life," says Grandmother Spider. "I must stir them every few moments so they may continue to grow throughout the earth, just as I weave the tapestry of the journey of life, death, and rebirth told within my web."

As if to demonstrate the validity of her explanation, Grandmother Spider turns and goes to the stone basin, the cauldron, and begins to slowly stir the seeds with an extended forelimb.

"Thank you, Grandmother," says Dragonfly as Grandmother Spider makes her way toward them again, standing before Dragonfly's face just as near as before. "Long must you have been here," continues Dragonfly; "weaving the beautiful tapestry and stirring the continuing of the seeds of life. Most gracious of you. I do have another question."

"Your flattery awarded you an answer to your first question, Dragonfly," says Grandmother Spider, tapping Dragonfly on top of his head with the same forelimb she used to stir the seeds. "The question is free; the answer comes with a price."

Grandmother Spider presses her face closer to Dragonfly's, waiting for him to speak; but Dragonfly does not speak, and Butterfly both hears and feels the rhythm within Dragonfly rise and fall and rise again, three times, then one, then two, another two times, and another two; and still, he does not speak.

Butterfly catches a glimpse of memory of when Dragonfly was but a water nymph and would descend beneath the surface of the water to blow his bubbles, then ascend again to speak or listen. She realizes he is contemplating; and this makes Butterfly smile, renews her vigor, vitality, and determination, as she continues to pluck away at the strand of web.

"Would you like to know the price for the answer to your question, Dragonfly?" asks Grandmother, her crone-voice cackling.

"Yes, Grandmother," says Dragonfly, without hesitation.

"You must be the one to choose, young and old Dragonfly of the in between," says Grandmother Spider as she takes a step back, raising herself higher. "Will you die first and give Butterfly those few more breaths of life and save yourself from the torment of having to watch her die? Or will she die first, award yourself a few more precious moments of life's breath, and thus, save her from the terror of watching you die? Which mercy will it be, Dragonfly?"

Again, Dragonfly alters his internal rhythm. Irregularly and then regularly again.

"I propose a trade, Grandmother," says Dragonfly. "A barter, a this for that."

"What do you propose, Dragonfly?" asks Grandmother Spider as she lowers herself, leaning closer to Dragonfly; her tone of voice seeming disappointed but curious to Butterfly.

"Take me," says Dragonfly. "Add my most magnificent colors to your tapestry of weaving. Let Butterfly yet live. She will stir the cauldron of the seeds of life for you; so that you may rest and wander. Perhaps leave the cave if you will; dive into the beauty of weaving your most beautiful web. Extend it further out of the cave and beyond while Butterfly tends the pot of seeds. The burden shared between the two, where you will then be as not two separate things."

Grandmother Spider rises, turns, and moves quickly, quicker than Butterfly would have thought possible, and stirs the cauldron of seeds; she stops and turns again, making her way back to where Dragonfly and Butterfly remain suspended; she pauses near a hanging cocoon of webbing, where one of her more recent victims shudders now and again, futilely attempting to escape its bonds; and she sinks her fangs into the plump body, quick as lightning, draining the fluids from whatever creature had been so entwined.

Butterfly's heart drops and her limb begins to shake, and she stops. She feels Dragonfly's internal rhythm shifting again, that irregular breath of pause for three and then one and then two; and then become regular, a repeat of two, and two, and two, and so on. She begins to match her own with his and her limbs calm, her focus steadies, and she continues the plucking of the thread.

Grandmother Spider scurries quickly—again, faster than Butterfly thought would be possible for her size and guessed-at age—straight before Dragonfly's face, their little micro hairs bristling against one another, they are so close. A viscous goo drips from her maw to the webbing and cave floor below.

"Are you asking, Dragonfly?" asks Grandmother Spider, her cackling crone-voice laced with a fatal invitation.

"I am suggesting," says Dragonfly, immediately.

"Clever boy," says Grandmother Spider.

"The choice is yours, Grandmother," says Dragonfly.

"You cannot trick a trickster, Dragonfly," says Grandmother Spider as she takes a step back, raising herself high, leaning forward, and putting all eight of her eyes directed at Dragonfly; the warning and intention clear—that she sees him.

"I would never presume to attempt, Grandmother," says Dragonfly, the reverence in his voice presenting the clear image of a bowed head, just as he would be doing if he were not held steadfast within the web. "I merely present possibility and opportunity."

"Better to ask forgiveness than permission, eh?" asks Grandmother Spider, seeming to calm and become at ease, tilting her head and entire body to one side as if something else caught her attention.

"Better to forgive and be forgiven, Grandmother," says Dragonfly, responding in kind and not skipping a beat.

"Who told you that?" asks Grandmother Spider, whipping her body around quickly, again facing Dragonfly with her full attention returned to him.

"The Wind," says Dragonfly.

"That blustering fool thinks it knows all," says Grandmother Spider, cackling, and turning toward the entrance of the cave and looking outward. "All air is the Wind, boy."

"That is what I like about it, Grandmother," says Dragonfly, as though he is pulling words from thought and memory whispering to him in that very moment. "It cannot be trapped or caught, and it goes where it pleases."

"It cannot go everywhere," says Grandmother Spider, bending down to Dragonfly's face with a menacing glare, daring him to challenge her claim at the cost of his life. "The Wind does not come into my cave and does not know the stories of the deep places in the dirt where it cannot reach."

"I can bring the Wind into your cave, Grandmother," says Dragonfly as he looks up into Grandmother Spider's eight eyes with his customary quizzical expression of curiosity and mischief.

Grandmother Spider is rocked back by Dragonfly's words, and she looks around the cave as if expecting the Wind to suddenly arrive.

"Telling lies, Dragonfly?" she asks with a mixture of threat and curiosity, pressing her face to his again.

"Never, Grandmother," says Dragonfly. "It is true. The Wind will blow, even here in this cave."

"Prove it," demands Grandmother Spider. "Bring the Wind, Dragonfly."

Dragonfly takes a visible breath, holds it for a few moments, and exhales slowly.

"The Wind is on its way, Grandmother," proclaims Dragonfly. "It will be here soon."

Grandmother Spider looks at Dragonfly suspiciously.

"How soon?" she asks.

Dragonfly takes another visible breath, holding it even longer before exhaling slowly.

"In the time it takes you to tell three stories from your weaving, Grandmother," says Dragonfly.

Grandmother Spider looks down upon her web of creation, turns, and scurries to the back of the cave where she stirs the cauldron of seeds; then moves with ferocious quickness to stand before Dragonfly again.

"I will tell you the three stories, and no more, Dragonfly," says Grandmother Spider. "If the Wind does not come after the third story, then I will take your wings for my tapestry, and your story will be told as that of a liar, traitor, and betrayer of your Butterfly friend—she who I will make my slave until she is too weak, and then I shall let my children feast upon her flesh. And only I and the dead here will know the truth. In the story, you will be the villain, and none save those who know how to see and read the web will know the truth of your true virtue. Do you accept the terms, Dragonfly?"

Dragonfly takes a deep breath, holding the inhale in even longer than the previous two times before exhaling; and again, Butterfly is reminded of the final bubbles Dragonfly had blown before he ascended the reed and made his transformation from nymph to Dragonfly, without hesitation but profound determination.

"I accept, Grandmother," says Dragonfly. "The Wind will come after the final story."

Grandmother Spider spins in a circle, scurries to the back of the cave, stirs the cauldron of seeds, and returns to Dragonfly. She spins another circle, a second, and then a third before folding her legs inward and settling into the web beneath her.

"The first story is that of the *Heyoka. Hoka Hey*," says Grandmother Spider, her words of narration echo and reverberate throughout body, cave, and the very threads of the web themselves, humming with sound in rhythm with the synergetic beating of hearts, and the rising and falling of breath emanating from the still living.

Butterfly continues to delicately pluck away at the thread of webbing holding Dragonfly's wing, feeling a sensational warm and electrified stillness as Grandmother Spider's crone-voice creates intricate images, patterns, and sceneries unlike anything she had ever seen or dreamed.

"Among the tribes of the two-legged walkers, there once was a young warrior who was also a trickster. One day, the young warrior came upon a storm and asked to be given the power of thunder and lightning.

The storm rumbled and spoke to the young warrior.

'You ask for great power and responsibility,' said the storm. 'What will you give in equal exchange for such a gift?'

The young warrior thought for a moment, as he was a trickster by nature, he was wary of making a deal with the unpredictable storm and thought it best to take a humble course and leave nothing to chance.

'I have not but my bow, arrow, my axe, and short knives,' said the young warrior. 'I have my senses, my hands, my feet, and my wits; and these I was given by the great spirit to hunt, protect, and make home, so you may not have them. What could I possibly give the most mighty and magnificent storm, wielder of wind, rain, thunder, and lightning, that you may share in your gifts, and that I may protect the tribes of the people against what not to do?'

The storm thundered, and a lightning bolt struck near to the warrior. The warrior nearly ran and fainted but knew that if the storm wished him dead by lightning, he would have been dead before he blinked; so, he did not move but bowed his head, looked up at the storm, and waited.

'It is not to me you must give, but to your mother,' said the storm. Return when you have given to her your heart.'

The young warrior bowed his head again and turned to go to his mother, his heart pounding heavily in his chest. He knew of how the ancient elements spoke in riddles but also knew their riddles were sometimes literal; he hoped this was not one of those times and that he would not have to open his chest to place his bleeding heart in his mother's hands. Surely, she would weep at such a thing. *That would be no grand gift,* he thought to himself. The young warrior breathed deeply, and behind him the storm rumbled with thunder and lightning streaking through the sky.

The warrior approached his mother and leaving out his deal with the storm for its thunder and lightning so as not to worry her, he told her he would like to give her a gift from his heart and asked what would make her happiest. The young warrior was a clever trickster and had surmised this is what the storm had meant by giving his mother his heart.

'Oh, how wonderful,' said the mother. 'I adore your drawings with the charcoal and ash. Draw pictures of the caterpillars for me, I would love that.'

The young warrior nodded, turned, and went to fetch charcoals from the fire and skins to draw upon. An easy enough gift, he thought, in return for the power of thunder and lightning.

As the young warrior sat and began to draw, he again and again discarded the pictures of the caterpillars he would draw, not satisfied with any of them. He grew so frustrated with failing at drawing a simple caterpillar that he decided to take a break and go hunting.

Many months passed as he tracked and hunted, and he nearly forgot about his deal with the storm and gift for his mother. The young warrior realized his heart was not in the drawing of the caterpillar and this would not do as equal exchange.

The phases of the moon came and went, seasons changed and returned, until the young warrior finally returned from his hunt.

'Dearest son, have you brought me the picture of the caterpillar?' asked the mother. 'I have been so anxious to see.'

The young warrior paused for only a moment, thinking of a quick story to tell her.

'No, Mother, I am sorry,' he said; 'I injured my hand on the hunt and am unable to draw with the charcoals in such detail to recreate the caterpillar just now. What is another gift might I give that would make you happy?'

'My son, you must take care of your hands,' said the mother. 'I adore your paintings with the dyes and colors. Would you paint the beautiful butterfly for me? I would adore that.'

The young warrior laid down the skins and meat he had brought back from the hunt at his mother's feet, nodded, turned to collect his dyes and went to find good stones to paint upon.

He sat and began to paint, collecting a growing pile of stones at his feet as he, again, discarded every painting, dissatisfied with each and every one.

He grew frustrated again and decided to go and run with the wild horses to take a break from the task.

The young warrior befriended a wild stallion, and together they ran and thundered their way across the nations, the plains, the prairies, through the forests and the swamps, up and around mountains to crystal clear lakes and rivers; and as fast as they were able, they ran, streaking across the country for a time uncountable, having many adventures and playing with mischief.

After a long while, the warrior returned, and his mother smiled at him as he rode upon the camp on his trusted friend and steed.

'Dearest son, you have been gone so long,' said the mother. 'Have you brought me the painting of the butterfly? I have been imagining the beautiful colors you would paint.'

The warrior hesitated for barely a moment, he had completely forgotten of his promise to paint the butterfly and of his deal with the storm, though the young warrior was as quick and clever as ever and thought of a story to tell her.

'No, Mother, I am sorry,' he said. 'I traveled far and wide to find the most beautiful colors to paint the butterfly for you; but I could not find the right ones. Is there another gift I might give that would make you happy?'

'My son, any color would have been as beautiful as another,' said the mother; 'you need not have gone so far out of your way to try and make it perfect for me; although, I do adore your music. Play a song for me, I would love that.'

The young warrior winced inside at her words, he knew he had not gone out of his way for her; he had forgotten after growing frustrated and became distracted with other things, his adventures, and all that he had done and learned. His heart was not in the painting, and he knew it would not do for equal exchange for the power of thunder and lightning.

The young warrior nodded and smiled, now determined to give this gift from his heart to his mother and claim his reward of thunder and lightning from the storm.

He collected his instrument and began to formulate a song, though every note escaped him, and no harmony or melody came to him that pleased him or that he felt within his heart.

And so, once again, frustrated, the young warrior heaved with a shout and flung his instrument as far from him as he could.

As the instrument disappeared into the reeds, a sweet sound fluttered through the air, a soft laughter that made his heart flutter and the small hairs all over his body stand on end. He turned, and there sat a beautiful woman of the people with feathers in her hair and eyes like piercing arrow heads.

The young warrior asked this woman to be his wife, and they travelled the lands together in loving embrace, enjoying countless new adventures, dancing their way through the seasons of change with songs in their hearts and upon their lips.

Many moons had passed before the warrior once again returned, and there sat his mother by her fire.

She looked up at him as he approached with his wild stallion friend and his beautiful wife by his side, and she smiled.

'Dearest Son, many moons have passed since last you were here,' said the mother. 'Have you brought me your song? I would love to hear.'

The young warrior's smile fell as he remembered he had completely forgotten, again, his promise to give his mother a gift from his heart; and once again, he thought quickly and cleverly.

'No, Mother, I am sorry,' he said. 'My instrument broke, and I have gathered everything I need to make a new one, but the tune is not ready. Is there another gift I might give you that would make you happy?'

'My son, you must take care of your instrument that moves your song through you,' said the mother. 'Hold it more gently and with care. I do adore the stories you tell by the fire. Write the story of the truth that is in your heart for me. I would love that.'

The young warrior's heart nearly leapt from his chest. It pounded so loudly it felt as if thunder were rumbling all around and through him. The small hairs upon his body stood tall, reaching for the sky, and tingling sensations like lightning coursed through him from head to toe and back up again. He nodded and said to himself, *yes! This is it!*

The young warrior turned and ran to fetch his writing tools and skins to write upon. He sat upon the earth, and he began to write without hesitation.

He wrote all that he had thought and learned, all that he had believed, all that he had known, unknown, and unlearned, all that he had found and come to believe; of every cup he emptied and filled, every bowl and vessel he broke and shattered, and those he mended.

He wrote of his adventures and his failings. He wrote of the lies he told, and was told, and of his truths; he wrote of beginnings, endings, and of the spaces in between; he wrote of meaning, of virtue, of fear.

He wrote all that he honored, held sacred, and most dear; he wrote of the all, of every connection he felt; and he wrote of love.

The young warrior leapt to his feet as he finished the final word, and without thinking he ran to give his mother this gift of the truth within his heart.

She sat there by the fire, and the young warrior presented the skins with his heartfelt words written upon them.

'Mother, I have told you the truth that is in my heart,' said the young warrior; 'and I have written it in the form of a story so that it may be shared, everlasting. I give it to you.'

The young warrior's mother turned from her task at the fire, looked at him, and smiled, and she held out her hands.

He placed the skins with the truth in his heart written upon them in her hands, and he sat and waited for her to read them.

To the warrior's surprise, his mother sat the skins down beside her and turned back to her task at the fire.

'I must finish my work,' she said; 'this day is not my own. I will read your words when I am finished.'

With a moment of disappointment but with understanding, the young warrior stood, turned, and went to reflect at the lake beneath the old willow tree.

The warrior sat there and investigated the surface of the waters as the sun set and the moon rose, now reflected onto the surface of the waters where the warrior had set his gaze. With a gentle breeze brushing the bows of the willow tree against his skin, the young warrior was roused from his reverie and reflection and went to see if his mother had read his words.

As he approached his mother, he noticed she did not turn to greet him with the cheerful smile as was her custom to do; instead, this time, she turned and began beating corn beside the fire in a wooden mortar.

As soon as she began beating the corn, a large pheasant was startled from the high grass, and the young warrior watched it disappear into the nearby woods; and the young warrior sat beside his mother and waited.

Without meeting his gaze, she held out an ear of corn to him.

'Do you want to help me beat this corn?' she asked with a strange jovial attitude and a shaking in her voice.

The young warrior cocked an eyebrow, gave a little laugh, and began beating the corn; as he did so, he heard a thumping and drumming sound coming from the wood where the pheasant had gone. A sound as though something was being beaten against a hollow log.

'There was much to do this day here,' said the mother, pulling the warriors attention back to her, the corn, and the fire. 'I have been so busy, and I am tired. How are you, son?

What did you do with your day?'

The young warrior cocked his eyebrow again and gave another short laugh.

'I wrote the truth that is in my heart and placed it in your hands as a gift,' said the young warrior.

'Oh, you wrote that today?' asked the mother, without any hesitation or turning to look at the young warrior, she simply continued beating the corn.

The young warrior had stopped, and again the thumping sound from the woods drew his attention.

'Yes,' said the young warrior. 'Did you read it?'

The young warrior then turned from the woods, looked to his mother, and glanced at the skins sitting beside her that held his words, the truth from his heart.

The mother stopped beating the corn, picked up the skins, and held them in her hands.

'Yes,' said the mother. 'I did.'

The young warrior looked at the skins with his words from his heart upon them.

'And?' he asked.

'I disagree,' said the mother as she gently placed the skins within the fire and went back to beating the corn.

The young warrior watched the flames engulf the skins as they curled and glowed bright and turned to blackened ash. He watched the embers flick and fly from the fire, up into the air. He continued to watch as they ascended toward the sky among the stars.

The warrior smiled, stood, and began walking from the fire.

The woods were silent. His mother paused from the work on the corn and looked up at the warrior.

'I love you, son,' said the mother.

The warrior turned and continued walking into the night.

'I love you too,' said the warrior.

The warrior continued walking until he at last came upon the storm. He stood tall and looked up at the storm as it rumbled lightly, flickers of light emanating from within the rolling clouds.

'You have returned,' said the storm. 'Have you given your mother your heart?'

The warrior bowed his head and returned his eyes to the storm.

'I have,' said the warrior. 'Though she did not accept it. She put it to the flame.'

'When the heart is given in truth, it is not often received,' said the storm. 'Even the power of a mother's love may not always overcome the fear of truth that is not ready to be accepted.'

'I have failed then,' said the young warrior, bowing his head again with a tear welling in his eye and rolling down his cheek.

The storm thundered loudly and then grew still and silent, the rolling clouds unmoving.

'No, young warrior,' said the storm. 'Though, you are too clever for your own good, sometimes. You have tricked yourself, trickster. And I confess, I played a trick myself. 'Tis our nature, after all. That which you have asked for is already within you.'

The warrior remained still before the storm, with his head bowed and tears formed in both eyes widely shut, falling, and cascading down his cheeks.

The clouds of the storm began to bellow and darken, changing shape and form, expanding, the winds howled around him, the rumbling growing from within.

The warrior raised his head and opened his eyes, the thunder boomed aloud, cacophonous, and earth-shattering, multitudes of lightning struck the ground all around again, and again, and again.

The darkness of the night was brought to life in abundant light, and the warrior smiled."

CHAPTER III – PART 2

Grandmother and the Weaving

G randmother Spider grows silent, she rises and turns to the back of the cave, moving slowly, and the single droplet of water from the cave ceiling falls into the cauldron of seeds as she begins to stir.

She makes her way back to stand before Dragonfly in still silence.

"What sadness, Grandmother," says Dragonfly.

"Sadness?" asks Grandmother, peering down with her eight eyes on Dragonfly. "Sadness for the young warrior?"

"For the mother," says Dragonfly.

Grandmother Spider says nothing as she folds in her legs and sits upon her webbing, the black orbs of her eyes glowing with the violet light of the cave fungi.

Butterfly continues to pluck away slowly and steadily at the strand of webbing holding onto Dragonfly's wing; and she dares not stop.

"And now for your second story, Dragonfly," says Grandmother Spider, the timber of her voice lowering, the reverberations echoing across the cave walls, into the webbing and weaving, and through their bodies as her words, again, become the voices and images in their minds. "This one is titled, 'Son of the Sun and Crow.'

Among the tribes of the two-legged peoples, there was a chief with hair the color of the crow. When this chief was young, he was a fierce and respected warrior and did many great deeds for his tribe and people.

While in his prime, this young chief was returning from a battle against the tribe of assassins, and while partaking in the sacred medicines and spirit waters, the chief fell from his horse and was injured in a way he would not recover from in wholeness.

Though he was able to remain as chief due to the respect the tribespeople had for him and his deeds, he could no longer adventure or go to war and battle as he had done before.

So, the chief became well-known and respected for being a giver of plenty. He held great reverence for the elders and the old traditions, even bringing back some of those old ways that had been close to forgotten. The chief's favorite tradition was that of the pipe and sacred tobacco and the telling of the stories of the people, which he shared openly and often.

Then came the day the chief took a wife, a pale-faced wife with hair the color of the midday-sun. The tribespeople accepted the chief's new wife, for even though her skin was pale, she held the same respect and love for the old traditions as did the chief, and this gave the tribe great comfort.

And so, when the sun-haired wife bore the chief a son, the people rejoiced and were glad.

The son of the chief grew, resembling both the sun-haired wife and the crow-haired chief, not entirely like one and not entirely like the other.

In the heat of the summer months, his hair was lighter like the sun-haired wife and his eyes were green like fresh spring leaves and the grass of the plains, and in the cold winter, his hair was darker like the crow-haired chief and his eyes the brown color of the standing people, the trunks of the trees of the forest.

The son grew up enjoying and learning all the old traditions and stories and honored them deeply. The chief and his wife were proud, and the tribe was glad.

Since the chief could not go out and hunt, battle, or adventure, the son had to learn of these things on his own and from others. What the son did learn from his father, the chief, was the honor and reverence and appreciation of all the stories.

The chief and the son would stay awake for days sharing the stories again and again over the passing of the pipe with tobacco. They particularly enjoyed the ghost stories.

Now, there was something peculiar about the son of the chief that sometimes would bring joy and sometimes frustration to the chief and his wife.

The son was overly inquisitive; he questioned absolutely everything he was told, unusually so to where it seemed as though no answer given would ever be sufficient or accepted.

Further, he was extremely exact and literal, which seemed to go against his need for questions.

The son of the chief seemed to both know nothing and have a question for everything, while at the same time he had an exact answer for everything and knew all. This would infuriate the chief, and he would ponder these peculiarities about his son many times while he partook with tobacco.

This peculiarity of the son and frustrated joy of the chief and his wife was announced one day when the son had barely seen but two changes of the seasons.

The chief lay upon the banks of a lake, partaking in his tobacco, and he watched his young son walk out among a fallen tree that floated upon the lake, reaching out into the deepest parts of the waters.

He cocked his head and watched as the child would walk up and down the fallen tree, dipping his toes into the water after every step. The child knew the water was deep, and he could not yet swim and had been told again and again not to go there, yet here he was, dipping his toes in the very place he was not supposed to be.

As the chief pondered, while taking turns on his tobacco, he thought to himself, *Is the boy testing the water, me, or his own courage?*

And then it happened suddenly, without even a shout, the son slipped and fell into the deep waters. Even with his old injuries, the chief leaped up, ran, dived into the waters, and pulled his young son from the lake and returned him to the shore, wrapping him in skins and building him a fire to warm him.

The chief then sat beside his son, who stared out at the water and into the fire. The chief laughed and shook his head at the child and reached for his pipe. Then he remembered he had it in his hands when he dove into the water.

The chief's son pointed his finger toward the lake and the fallen tree, and the chief looked, and there was his broken tobacco pipe, just then sinking beneath the surface of the lake.

The chief shrugged his shoulders, shook his head, laughed, and lay on his back beside his young son and looked up at the sky as the stars began to shine and appear.

Many years later, it was another such occurrence of the son seeming to know nothing and everything that would cause a huge rift between he and the chief and split the tribe in two.

The son was now a man, and his questions were no longer questions of a curious child but perplexing, provoking; and drove the chief to stay within his lodge, smoking his tobacco for long periods of time, to escape his son's seemingly endless interrogations.

One day the son went into the chief's lodge where he was partaking his tobacco.

'Father why are the tribes of the plains and the tribes of the mountains still at war?' asked the son.

The chief took two turns with the tobacco before handing the pipe to his son.

'You know this story already, my son,' said the chief. 'It is one of the first you learned as a child. We have spoken of it many times.'

The son took a single turn of the tobacco and returned the pipe to the chief.

'Perhaps we go over it one more time, Father,' said the son; and we see what may be learned as to why we are still at war over a story that is now centuries old and that was forgotten and then remembered more times than can be counted.'

The chief took three turns with the tobacco while he contemplated, as the chief enjoyed the old stories as much as he enjoyed his tobacco. He relented to the inquisitive request, and he handed the pipe to his son.

'Very well,' said the chief. 'It is a good story to be told, anyway. I will begin.'

Before the chief could begin the story, the son put up his hands in humble refusal of the offered pipe.

'What if we tell the story differently this time?' asked the son. 'We will take turns and share our remembering of its telling. You begin, and then I will speak, and then back to you. Where you tell of the beginning, Father, I will tell of the ending.'

The chief eyed his son suspiciously as he took two turns of the tobacco, considering this new way of telling. The chief was not fond of change, especially changes to his stories and the ways they were told. He again moved to hand the pipe to his son, and again the son humbly refused.

At the second refusal of the pipe, the chief took offense.

'Do you no longer revere the sacred tobacco and wish to partake with your father, the chief?' asked the chief.

The son raised his eyebrow, looking at the pipe as the chief added more tobacco to it and then back at his father.

'Of course, I do, Father, chief,' said the son. 'I have a great and meaningful love for both. I simply enjoy the single turn the same as you enjoy many.'

The chief took a single turn of the tobacco, though it was long and slow, and the smoke grew thick and heavy within the chief's lodge.

'Let us tell the story of the division of the tribes,' said the chief.

The chief took another single turn of the tobacco, adding to the thickness of the permeating smoke.

'Long ago the people were of one nation spread across the land. There is a meeting place at the base of the great peak, a sacred place where the people would hold council before the banks of the medicine waters.

One day two hunters from neighboring tribes, one of the plains and one of the mountains, stopped at the meeting place on their return from a hunt to rest and drink of the healing medicine waters.'

The chief paused and took a turn of his tobacco; but he did not offer the pipe to his son; and the son took a deep breath.

'As the two hunters arrived at the meeting place, it was clear only one of them had been successful on the hunt,' said the son.

'As one laid down a fat deer, the other looked at it with jealousy, and when the successful hunter bent over the medicine waters and poured a handful of it on the ground in honor of the great spirit, the other hunter spat words with venom in his heart.'

The son paused, took a breath, and looked at his father, offering him the turn to continue the story as if he were passing the pipe of tobacco.

'Why does a stranger drink the medicine waters that his children may drink it undefiled?' said the chief.

'I am chief of my tribe, and I drink at the headwater. We are one nation. Let us drink together,' said the son, before the chief could continue.

The son again paused, took a breath, and looked to his father, offering the turn. The chief held the silent pause and took a turn of the tobacco pipe.

'No. Your tribe pays tribute to mine, and I lead the nation to war. I am chief of my people the same as I am chief of yours,' said the chief, then pausing and taking two turns of the tobacco, as the son waited for his father to finish and let the smoke billow between them.

'Lies,' said the son. 'Your tongue is forked, like the snake's. Your heart is black. When the Great Spirit made his children, he did not say to one, drink here and to another, drink there but gave water that all might drink.'

The son paused and took a deep breath; and the chief took a single turn of the tobacco.

'The other hunter made no answer to this, and the successful hunter bent to press his lips to the surface of the medicine waters to drink,' said the chief; 'as he did so, the other hunter came up behind him. He leaped upon him and drove his head beneath the water, holding him there until he was drowned.'

The chief paused, took two turns of his tobacco; and the son waited for the chief to release the cloud of smoke.

'As the other hunter pulled the dead body from the waters,' said the son; 'the surface became agitated, bubbling and boiling, and from there arose a vapor, a steam that became the form of one of the venerable people, a man with long, white locks, whom the other hunter, now murderer, recognized as the father of the one nation.

A man whose heroism and good deeds had made his name and visage revered through all the tribes in the nation. The face of the patriarch was dark and full of wrath as he looked upon the now-murderer.'

The son stopped speaking and breathed in deeply and exhaled. The chief met his son's gaze and then lowered it to the pipe. He took a single short turn, and the smoke escaped his nostrils.

'The ancestor then spoke in terrible tones,' said the chief, puffing out his chest and lowering his head to imitate the visage and tone of the enraged patriarch. *'Accursed of my race! This day thou hast severed the mightiest nation in the world. The blood of the brave appeals for vengeance. May the water of thy tribe be rank and bitter in their throats.'*

The chief then took another short turn from the tobacco and let the smoke escape his nostrils as he kept his gaze upon the pipe.

'After speaking the final word of the curse,' said the son; 'the ancestor raised up an elk-horn club and brought it smashing down on the head of the now-murderer, whose head was burst open, and he fell into the medicine waters, dead, turning them polluted and undrinkable, as they remain to this day.'

The son opened his mouth to continue with the story but then paused, looked at his father, who was taking another turn of his tobacco, and instead took a breath and offered his father, the chief, the next turn in telling. The chief noticed this and took another turn of his tobacco. He closed his eyes and let the smoke escape from both his lips and nostrils.

'In memory of the chief who said the waters were for all to drink, the great spirit smote a nearby boulder,' said the chief; 'and from within it rushed forth a fountain of delicious water.'

The chief took a long turn of the tobacco and let out three rings of smoke one after the other.

The son watched his father create the smoke rings and reflected on, yet another skill not cultivated and passed on to him by his father, the chief.

A small and arbitrary one, but another one all the same; and the son took a deep breath.

'The bodies of the two hunter chiefs were found by the people and the partisans began,' said the son; 'and on that day started the long and destructive war, which infected the other tribes one after the other. Lines were drawn upon the land; the one nation became many. The once-connected tribes now became separate just as the mountains became separate from the plains. The People were now in division.'*

The chief brought his pipe to his lips but paused and looked to his son.

'You changed some of the telling of the tale,' said the chief.

'I did,' said the son, while the chief took a single turn of the tobacco. 'I also kept some of the same. I ask again, why the tribes are still at war?'

'Because some tribes seek to dominate the others,' said the chief, responding with the same answer he had always given to all, and any, who he told this story to for as long as the son could remember.

'Why do we not attempt to unite the tribes as one nation?' asked the son.

'All tribes would have to want to be one nation to be one nation.' said the chief, another of the predetermined responses the son has always heard.

'What if they do, but they have forgotten and need only a reminder why they want to be one nation?' asked the son.

The chief paused and took two turns of his tobacco.

'The tribes are too divided and set in their own ways,' said the chief. 'It is what it is.'

The son waited as the chief took three full turns of the tobacco.

'What if we can change what is?' asked the son.

'We cannot,' said the chief, taking a single turn of the tobacco.

The son closed his eyes, took a long, deep breath, pausing for an extended amount of time in between the inhale and exhale. So long, even the chief took notice. After exhaling his breath, the son opened his eyes and looked at his father.

'What if enough of us dare to hope?' asked the son; 'To dream, and to believe we can change what is?'

The chief sighed in frustration and shook his head.

'No,' said the chief. 'It is not possible.'

'Why do you doubt that, together, we can make the impossible, possible?' asked the son.

'Because I am your father and the chief,' said the chief. 'Because I say so, I know so; and you will respect me and what is.'

The chief was unable to hold in his agitation with being continuously questioned by his son any longer and wished to be done with the conversation

The son cocked his eyebrow at his father and took three breaths while the chief added more tobacco to his pipe.

'I hold utmost respect for you, Father,' said the son; 'but you being my father has nothing to do with what is or what may be; in fact, it means little to most, if not all, save me, that you are my father. I say this to you now from my respect and honor of all things—Father, you have not been a true chief for many years.'

The chief sat up straight and puffed out his chest and glowered at his son who sat across from him.

'Here it is, then,' said the chief. 'I know your true intent. You wish to be chief now of my tribe. I do not wish to hear your reasons and questions of why, I already know what you are after. I have always known.'

The son closed his eyes and took three short but deliberate breaths; and he opened his eyes.

'If you do not wish to hear what I have to say and you already know, then why would we speak at all?' asked the son.

The chief took a single turn of the tobacco, nodded, took another turn of the tobacco.

'Speak, then,' said the chief.

The son took a single breath as the chief continued to take short turns of the tobacco.

'Father. I am a chief,' said the son. 'I have been for quite a while now. Also, I am a father of many children. I have been traveling and journeying. I have been mending the bonds once broken so long ago in the bloodlines. I speak with the ancestors and carry the flame for the reconnection of the people of the nation. I am here asking you to return to the one nation. You have been here in your lodge so long, partaking in tobacco and sacred medicines for an entire age, clinging to your ancient injuries, that you have not partaken in life. You are disconnected from it, from yourself, from your wife, my mother, from me and your descendants, from the people, from the ancestors, from the land, and from the spirit.'

The chief breathed heavily through his nostrils and glared at his son.

'You speak as the fork-tongued snake from the story,' said the chief through gritted teeth. 'Without reverence or respect for me, your father. I am the one who brought the remembrance of the stories back to the people. I speak to the ancestors, always, with the sacred tobacco medicine.'

The son closed his eyes and bowed and shook his head. He took a deep breath, raised his head, and then opened his eyes, looking at his father.

'No, Father,' said the son. 'The only thing you commune with in your overconsumption of tobacco and medicines is distraction and pain. And it has made you forgetful and bitter.'

The chief nearly stood up as his son finished those last words. He glared at his son and pointed his tobacco pipe at him.

"I will not listen to your disrespectful words any longer,' said the chief. 'You think yourself so clever, that you know everything, when you know nothing. You have no respect for me as your father, and I will not speak to you until you do!"

The Chief pointed his pipe away from his son, toward the outside, and nodded at it. Then he began packing more tobacco into it and did not remove his eyes from the pipe.

The son glanced at the skin covering the lodge's singular entrance and exit and then looked back at his father. He watched him pack the tobacco; he watched the embers flare, catch, and the smoke begin to whirl; he watched his father press the pipe to his lips and take his turn with his medicine.

The son closed his eyes and took a deep breath. He looked a final time at his father, who would not meet his gaze, and then he turned and left his father's lodge, a cloud of smoke following him into the open air of the outside and ascending toward the stars that had just begun to shine and appear in the sky.

The son of the chief stood tall and looked up into the sky and then before him, where the people stood waiting for him. As he walked forward, they each placed a hand upon his shoulder. They handed him a torch enflamed with glowing light, blue in its core.

He grasped it in his hand, holding it high, and with this light, he guided the people of the tribes away from the stagnant, smoking lodge and out into the nation."

CHAPTER III – PART 3

Grandmother and the Weaving

Grandmother Spider, again, grows silent as she slowly rises, turns, goes to the back of the cave, stirs the cauldron of seeds, and then makes her way back to stand before Dragonfly.

"What stubbornness, Grandmother," says Dragonfly.

"Stubborn?" asks Grandmother Spider, peering down, again, at Dragonfly with her shining eight eyes. "The father or the son?"

"Both," says Dragonfly.

Grandmother Spider says nothing as she spins, deliberately, in a circle and then folds in her limbs, and she lowers herself to sit upon the webbing.

"Dragonfly, here is your third and final story," says Grandmother Spider. "And then, for your sake, I do hope the Wind does appear as you have promised."

"The Wind will blow, Grandmother," says Dragonfly, matching Grandmother Spiders soft and deliberate tone.

Grandmother Spider says nothing for a few moments as Butterfly finds herself implementing the irregular breathing pattern, she learned from feeling Dragonfly's contemplative rhythm, so the fear that is coursing through her does not give her pause in her work at plucking away at the thread of webbing.

She gives great attention to moving from irregular to regular, as she hears Grandmother Spider's voice taking on that dreamlike trance as she descends into the third and final story telling.

"This story is titled, The Feathered One's Dance," says Grandmother Spider.

"Once, there was a hunter of the two-legged people who heard a noise in the night that was like the swooping wind of a storm and a great thunderous flapping.

The hunter rushed outside his tepee, expecting to see a great and terrible storm cloud approaching, and instead found a giant eagle perched atop the rack, feasting on the deer he had shot that day. Without hesitating, the hunter knocked arrow to bow, let fly, and shot the giant eagle through the heart, and it fell to the ground, dead.

As the hunter watched the eagle fall to the ground, he thought he could hear the distant rumbling of thunder. He stood a moment, listening, but heard nothing; and he returned to his tepee and slept.

In the morning, the hunter packed his camp, he left the eagle laying in the dirt with the arrow still protruding from its chest, and he carried the deer back to his tribe.

He told the chief how he shot the deer and then when the eagle came, he shot the eagle and left it where it fell.

The chief told the hunter to take a band of men and go collect the eagle and bring it back, that they would have an Eagle Dance.

Before the hunter could move or blink, there was a deafening roar of thunder and lightning streaking across the sky, followed by a loud whoop.

From the woods where the whoop sounded, there emerged a strange warrior with many feathers of all cuts and colors.

In one hand the stranger carried the dead eagle the hunter had shot, and in the other hand, he held the hunter's arrow.

'Where is the brave warrior who has slain this eagle?' asked the stranger as he approached.

The chief said not a word and looked at the stranger. The hunter looked at the chief and then the stranger and stepped forward boldly.

'I shot the eagle as it was feasting upon the deer I shot,' said the hunter.

'Most mighty hunter,' said the stranger, raising the dead eagle before him; 'here is your prize you left behind in haste.'

'We are to have an Eagle's Dance," stammered the hunter as the stranger thrust the eagle into the arms of the hunter.

'Yes!' proclaimed the stranger, lifting the arrow into the air. 'The Dance of the Feathered Ones! And if your chief will permit it, in honor of your killing of the eagle, I shall dance within the circle and sing three songs of story as tribute!'

The stranger then looked at the chief with the arrow still raised in the air. The chief nodded and sent the hunter to prepare the circle and gather the tribe.

Night came, and the fires were lit, and the circle made. The feathered stranger stood in the center with the arrow still clutched in his hand.

The sound of the drums began, and the seven men holding the rattles led the Eagle's

Dance.

The stranger began to dance within the circle; he sang and chanted with the sounds of the rattles and drums.

'How the World was made,' sang the stranger.

'The earth is a floating island in a sea.

At each of the four corners is a cord that hangs down from the sky.

The sky is of solid rock.

When the world grows old and is worn out, the cords will break.

The earth will sink into the sea.

Everything will be water again, and the people will all be dead.

In the long time ago, when everything was water, when all the animals lived up in Galun'lati—

Beyond the stone arch that made the sky, it was very crowded, and all the animals wanted more room.

They wondered what was below the water.

At last Beaver's grandchild, the little Water Beetle, offered to run and find out.

Water Beetle darted all over the surface of the water but found no place to rest.

There was no land.

Water Beetle dived deep to the bottom and brought up some soft mud.

The mud began to grow and spread until it became the island that we call Earth.

The Earth was fastened to the sky with four cords, but no one remembers who did this.'

The stranger suddenly thrust the arrow into the sky. Thunder roared and crashed, and lightning struck the ground in the woods.

'Hi!' shouted the stranger, and as soon as the stranger shouted, one of the men with rattles, who was leading the dance, fell down dead; and the stranger continued his dance.

'At first the earth was flat, soft, and wet,' sang the stranger.

'The animals were anxious and sent the feathered ones to see.

But there was no place to land, so the feathered ones returned to Galun'lati.

Then the animals sent Buzzard and told him to go make ready for them.

The Great Buzzard, father of all the buzzards seen, flew all over the earth.

He flew low to the soft earth and grew tired.

His wings began to strike the ground.

Wherever they hit the earth, there was a valley made.

Whenever his wings moved upward there was made a mountain.

The animals saw this and were afraid the whole world would be mountains.

So, they called Buzzard back to Galun'lati.

When the earth became dry and the animals came down, it was dark.

So, the animals got the sun and set it into the sky and bid it go— every day—across the island from east to west, just over their heads.

It was too hot in that way, and Red Crawfish had his shell burned bright red.

The meat was spoiled, and the people did not eat of it.

Then the medicine men came and raised the sun a handsbreadth in the air, but it was still too scorching.

They raised it another time, and another time, until at last, they had raised it seven handsbreadths.

The sun rested just under the sky arch, and it was right, so they left it so.

Therefore, the medicine men called the high place, The Seventh Height.

Every day the sun goes along, under the arch and on the underside.

It returns at night on the upper side of the arch and back to its starting place.'

Once again, the stranger thrusted the arrow into the sky, thunder boomed and crashed, and lightning struck the ground in the nearby forest.

'Hi!' shouted the stranger, and with that shout, another of the men with a rattle fell dead; and the stranger continued his dance.

'There is another world under this earth,' sang the stranger.

'It is like this one in every way.

The animals, the plants, and the people—all are the same.

But the seasons are different.

The streams that come down from mountains, they are how we reach this underworld.

The springs at their heads are the doorways by which we enter.

To enter the other world, one must fast and then go to the water and have one of the underground people for a guide.

In the underworld, the water in the spring is always warmer in winter than the air in the above world.

And in summer, the water is cooler than the air in the above world.

We do not know who made the first plants and animals.

When they were made, they were told to watch and keep awake for seven nights.

And this is the way the young do now when they fast and pray to their medicine.

They tried to do this.

On the first night, nearly all the animals stayed awake.

On the second night, several of them fell asleep.

On the third night, more went to sleep.

Finally, on the seventh night, there was only the Owl and the Panther and one or two more who were still awake.

And so, these were given the power to see in the dark, to go about as if it were day, and to kill and eat the birds and animals that must sleep during the nighttime.

So, too, some of the trees fell asleep.

Only the cedar, the pine, the spruce, the holly, and the laurel were awake all seven nights.

And so, they are always green.

They are the sacred trees.

To all other trees it was said, *because you did not stay awake, you shall lose your hair every winter.*

After the plants and the animals, men came to the earth.

At first, it was one man and one woman only.

The man hit the woman with a fish, and in seven days, a child came down to the earth.

And so, came people to the earth.

They came so rapidly and quickly and fully, that it seemed the earth could not hold them all." *

For the third time, the stranger thrust the arrow into the sky, thunder crashed, and lightning struck the ground in the nearby wood.

'Hi!' shouted the stranger, and again, another man with a rattle fell dead. The people were frightened, but the drums and rattles continued, and the stranger began his second dance.

'The First Fire!' sang the stranger.

'In the beginning there was no fire, and the world was cold.

The Thunders, who lived in Galun'lati, sent Lightning, and put Fire in the hollow of a Sycamore tree that was growing on an island.

The animals could see the smoke but could not get to it because of the great water, so they held a council.

And this was long, long ago.

Every animal was anxious of the fire.

Raven offered first. He was large and strong.

He flew high and far across the water and landed upon the sycamore tree.

He was wondering what to do next when he looked at himself.

The heat had turned his feathers black.

Raven became so frightened; he flew back without any fire.

Screech Owl offered to go next.

He flew high and far across the water and landed upon a hollow tree.

As he was wondering what to do next, a blast of hot hair came forth and hurt his eyes.

Screech Owl became frightened, and he flew back, barely able to see.

And that is why the screech owl's eyes are red to this day.

The Hooting Owl and the Horned Owl went after.

By the time they reached the Sycamore tree, the fire burned so fiercely that the smoke nearly blinded them.

The ashes carried upon the breeze, made white rings around their eyes.

They returned without fire.

And so, they have white rings around their eyes to this day.

None of the feathered ones would go to the fire.'

For the fourth time, the stranger thrust the arrow into the sky. Thunder rumbled, roared, and crashed; and lightning struck the ground in the nearby forest.

'Hi!' shouted the stranger, and again, with the stranger's shout, another man with a rattle fell down dead; and the stranger continued his dance.

'The racer snake said he would go through the water and bring back fire,' sang the stranger.

'He swam to the island and crawled through the grass to the Sycamore tree.

He went into the tree by a hole in the bottom.

The heat and smoke were unbearable, and the ground at the bottom of the tree was covered in hot ashes.

The racer went back and forth, trying to get the ashes off.

At last, it managed to escape through the same hole it had entered, but his body had been burned completely black.

And now the racer snake is the Black Racer.

And that is why the Black Racer darts around and doubles back on its track, as if trying to escape.

Then, Great Blacksnake, the climber, offered to go for the fire.

Blacksnake was much larger than Black Racer.

So, Blacksnake swam over to the island and climbed up the Sycamore, as Blacksnake always does.

But when he poked his head into the hole, the smoke choked him, and he fell into the stump.

And he, too, was burned black.

So, the feathered ones and the animals and the snakes held council.

The world was still, very cold.

There was no fire.

The feathered, the crawlers, and the four-footed all refused to go for the fire.

They were all afraid of the burning sycamore tree.

Then it was Water Spider who said she would go.

Not the water spider that looks like mosquito.

Water Spider with black, downy hair and red stripes on her body.

She can run on top of the water and dive deep to the bottom.

The animals asked, *how can you bring back fire?*

Water Spider said not a word.

She spun a thread from her body, wove it into a tusti bowl and placed it upon her back.

She swam over to the island, then moved through the grass to the fire.

Water Spider put one single coal of fire into her tusti bowl and swam back with it.

And that is how fire came to the world.

And that is why Water Spider has a tusti bowl on her back." *

For the fifth time, the stranger raised the arrow into the sky. Thunder crashed and boomed, and lightning struck the ground in the nearby woods.

'Hi!' shouted the stranger, and again, as he shouted, a fifth man with a rattle fell dead.

The people were now very frightened, but the drums and rattles continued as the chief still sat and watched, never taking his eyes from the stranger, who began dancing again within the circle, his third and final dance.

'Medicine!' sang the stranger.

'The Old Ones say that at one time all of creation spoke the same language.

The plants could communicate with the finned ones.

The four-legged could speak with the trees.

The stones could talk to the wind.

And even the most dependent part of creation, the two-legged people, could also speak

45

with all the other parts of creation.

All existed in harmony.

The plants, the animals, and the elements of the Four Directions, of all existence.

All knew that if the two-legged were to survive, they would need help.

The animals gave of themselves, willingly sacrificing so the two-legged people could have food.

They knew their skins were much better for survival, so they allowed their skins to be taken and used for clothing and shelter.

The finned ones, the fliers and feathered ones, and the crawlers allowed themselves to be used by the two-legged people to insure their survival.

The plant people, the standing people of the trees, and the stone people of the rocks freely gave of themselves.

So, the two-legged people had what they needed for food, clothing, and shelter.

An agreement was forged that the two-legged peoples would ask permission for these gifts, give thanks for the sacrifice, and take no more than they needed.

And so, it was good.

But then, the two-legged peoples started growing in numbers rapidly and began to feel themselves more important than the rest of creation.

They began to believe that the Web of Life revolved around them.

They ignored the fact that they were just one small part of the Circle.

The two-legged peoples began to kill without asking permission.

They began to take more than what was needed.

They ceased to give thanks.

All parts of the agreement were broken.'

And for the sixth time, the stranger thrust the arrow to the sky, thunder boomed and crashed, and lightning struck the ground in the nearby forest.

'Hi!' shouted the stranger; and a sixth man with a rattle fell dead; and the stranger continued his dance.

'The great animal councils came together,' sang the stranger; 'to determine what to do, to right these wrongs.

They must protect themselves from destruction and eradication.

So, it was decreed, by Council, if one of their clans were killed by the two-legged people and thanks had not been given for the sacrifice—The Chief Animal Spirit would afflict the disrespectful killer with a devastating disease.

The plant people became distressed and said to the animals:

They wrong us too.

They dig us up, trample us, burn us out, and do not even listen when we try to tell them what we can do to help them.

Yet we feel compassion for the two-legged peoples.

The people struggle to realize their place in the web of creation, and they cannot learn if they are wiped out by disease.

They need our help.

So, for every disease you animal-peoples bring to them, we, the plant people will give them a cure.

All the two-legged people must do is listen when we talk to them. *

For the seventh time, the stranger thrust the arrow to the sky, and the thunder boomed and crashed louder and longer than any of the times before, the lightning bolt struck the ground in the forest and set a tree ablaze.

'Hi!' shouted the stranger; and so, the seventh man with a rattle fell dead.

Now all seven men who had rattles, who were leading the dance, were dead on the ground.

The people were too frightened to move; and the stranger looked to the sky and then thrust the arrow into the ground where he stood.

Rain fell from the dark clouds and put the fire in the forest out, and the stranger vanished into the darkness.

As the rain stopped, the moon began to shine, and the people started to move again. The hunter approached the chief, still holding the dead eagle.

'Who was that stranger?' asked the hunter.

The chief did not take his eyes from the arrow still pierced into the ground.

'That was the elder brother of the eagle you killed,' said the chief; 'without asking permission or giving thanks and left dead upon the ground with your arrow still in its heart.'*

Grandmother Spider slowly and silently rises, unfolding and extending her limbs, she turns and makes her way to the back of the cave and begins stirring the cauldron of seeds.

Butterfly continues plucking away at the thread of webbing while moving from her irregular to regular breathing rhythm. The vibrations coming through the webbing are noticeably intensified, the entire web is throbbing and humming.

Grandmother Spider is still with her back turned to them, ever so slowly turning the cauldron of seeds.

"Where is your friend, the Wind, Dragonfly?" asks Grandmother Spider, without turning around.

Butterfly feels Dragonfly's internal rhythm slow to a near halt. It rises and holds, and she almost stops to look and see if he still lives, and then she feels the descent.

"Grandmother, I am ready to ask my question," says Dragonfly.

Grandmother Spider pauses in her stirring of the seeds, and without turning, she continues stirring, the throbbing vibrations throughout the webbing intensifying from moment to moment. Butterfly plucks at the thread as steadily fast as she is able without breaking the rhythm.

"Ask your question, Dragonfly," says Grandmother Spider, her crone-voice barely above a whisper.

Time seems to slow as Dragonfly's breath becomes slow and steady, rhythmic, and regular.

"Grandmother," says Dragonfly. "If you had to choose between this or that, would you save the seeds or your unborn children?"

Deeper do the vibrations intensify throughout the webbing, visibly humming. The entire cave is alive with electric activity, the vibrations sending the gleaming lavender glows upon the silky threads, moving across the pattern of the web. Up and down, left, and right, all happening in an instant. Grandmother Spider has stopped stirring the seeds. She turns to face Dragonfly, her eight eyes wild with rage. She crouches her limbs, her maw agape and dripping. Butterfly remains focused on her steady task as the web jolts to life around her as Grandmother Spider leaps forward in her pounce of death.

Her arachnid legs leave the web, and she is suspended in the air, the thread snaps between Butterfly and Dragonfly, and his wing breaks free. In that very instant, Dragonfly rolls and spins, his four wings thunder to life, and the cave is cacophonous with the sounds of the storm and Wind. Dragonfly has brought the Wind beneath the earth.

Rising into the cave with furious wings of flight, he darts and dashes between the hanging threads and begins to circle and circle around and around the cave, so ferociously fast, the webbing begins to shred, tear, and follow in his wake.

Grandmother Spider crouches above the cauldron of seeds, shielding them with her body as she watches Dragonfly destroy her weaving, rising to the caves ceiling, the webbing a funneling tornado extending from Dragonfly, as if emanating from his tail. He dives straight toward Grandmother Spider and with a blast of wind sends the webbing toward her and then spins and rolls around, ripping Butterfly from the grasp of the webbing that held her and makes his way toward the cave's entrance, with her in his arms, as fast as his wings will carry him.

As he approaches the exit of the cave, he risks a glance back, expecting to see Grandmother Spider bounding after them. In truth, he expected to see her fangs and maw closing on him as soon as he looked, but instead, he sees a most curious sight.

Instead of a deadly spider pursuing him, he sees Grandmother crouched and spinning an entirely new web and weaving from the beginning, this one already a shinier and silkier pattern of threads and patterns that is even more amazing, wondrous, and beautiful than the one before.

Dragonfly can feel the vibrations and the rhythmic humming emanating from the story she has begun to weave as he makes his way out of her cave. If he is not mistaken, he is quite certain he hears Grandmother Spider humming and singing a song. He may never know for sure, but he will always wonder, as he looks upon her face a final time, *is that what a spider's smiling smirk looks like?*

Dragonfly zooms out of the cave and into the fresh air of the river's bank. The morning sun has just begun to rise, and there is the soft glow of the dawn's light to greet them. Dragonfly lands upon a nearby rock and helps Butterfly remove the rest of the webbing from her wings.

They say nothing as they remove the last of the old web from themselves and enjoy the coming light of the rising sun.

Butterfly turns and looks back toward where Grandmother Spider's cave resides.

"Why would she choose to save the seeds over her eggs—her unborn children?" asks Butterfly, breaking the silence.

Dragonfly stands beside Butterfly, looking in the same direction.

"Those seeds are the stories that make the world," says Dragonfly. "Without the stories there would be no time, no life, no world for the children to be born into."

Butterfly ponders this for a moment.

"Couldn't she have just gotten more seeds to replace them?" she asks.

Butterfly's concentration is broken as Dragonfly starts laughing nearly hysterically. Butterfly turns and looks at him with sternness but curiosity.

"Why are you laughing?" she asks.

His hysterics subside, but still chuckling to himself he turns from the direction of the cave and looks out at the river in the direction they are going.

"Because, Butterfly," he says; "if those seeds were so easily replaced, we would be dead right now."

Dragonfly shakes and flaps his wings, stretching out the last of the sticky webbing from the in-between places, cracks, and crevices.

Butterfly hesitates and watches Dragonfly as his laughter and chuckling dissipates, and he holds himself in stillness.

She reaches out and feels that internal rhythm irregular and regular emanating from within him.

"Dragonfly, the eggs," says Butterfly; "the unborn ones. Did you destroy them?"

Dragonfly continues to stare out at the river ahead of them, waiting for a moment to pass.

"Don't fret, Butterfly," he says. "They will yet be born into this world one day."

"They are safe, then, nestled in their fuzzy little sacs?" asks Butterfly, unable to help herself prying further into the wound.

"I cannot say for certain," says Dragonfly, turning to Butterfly with a flicking of his wings. "Although Grandmother Spider knew, as well as I, that I meant those eggs no harm."

"How do you know that?" asks Butterfly, shocked by his bold statement.

"Because you can't trick a trickster," says Dragonfly, chuckling to himself and turning back toward the rivers bend ahead of them.

"Then those seeds could have been replaced?" asks Butterfly, ignoring Dragonfly's evasive tactic. "Why did she protect them and not the eggs, and not attack us?"

"Not those particular seeds," says Dragonfly with a heavy sigh. "Others, perhaps, but not those very ones. And do not think for a moment that those eggs would not have hatched into hundreds of death-dealing infants that would have devoured you in a heartbeat. It would not have been an enjoyable experience, Butterfly. Trust me. A predator knows and a predator I am. Remember?"

"That doesn't matter, Dragonfly," says Butterfly quickly.

"Of course, it matters, Butterfly," says Dragonfly, half turning back, just enough to look directly in her eyes. "Every *thing* matters to *everything* and *everything* matters to every *thing*. Whether we or they see it or not, acknowledge it or not; or like it or not, it does. Everything is affected by everything else, all the way and all the time. So yes, it matters."

"How do you know it matters?" asks Butterfly, feeling uncertain.

"Because everything has a price," says Dragonfly, turning back to the river ahead, taking a breath and pause. "Today it was in our favor; tomorrow it may be in their favor. There is always a cost. An equal exchange. And you shall know it when it arrives. You can't get away with life, Butterfly, or away from death."

Butterfly listens and hears Dragonfly's words, and she feels both more certain and uncertain at the same time. She notices a strange sensation as she becomes aware of this. A feeling of quickening and lightening and being still and all she can think to herself is, what a curious feeling, and she laughs to herself at the reflection she has begun to see within herself.

"But why did Grandmother Spider spare us?" asks Butterfly, the question nagging at the back of her mind, stuck in her thoughts as if by those powerful strands of webbing. "If she need not protect either the eggs or seeds and could have spared both by simply destroying you, why didn't she?"

"Do you want to go back and ask her?" asks Dragonfly, without hesitating.

"No," says Butterfly, shuddering at the thought and memory of Grandmother Spider's cave and great web.

Dragonfly chuckles softly as he excites his wings into flight and hovers over the rock they are resting upon.

"Then don't fret," he says. "And let us continue. We'll add it to the list of questions for the Wind."

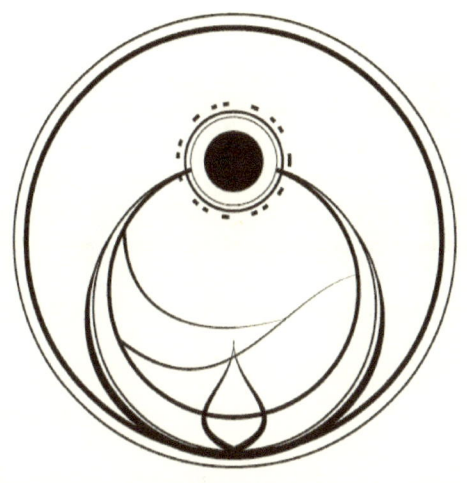

CHAPTER IV

Uncle and the Conquering of the Sun

Butterfly and Dragonfly travel the river straight through the morning, speaking little and doing everything they can to travel as fast and as far as they may from the memories of Grandmother Spider's cave and the thoughts of what almost became their fate within.

"I'm hungry," says Dragonfly, breaking the long silence as he hovers next to Butterfly.

"Again?" asks Butterfly, realizing she, too, is famished and cannot remember the last time she had eaten. "We just flew threw a swarm of river gnats. Did you not get your fill?"

"We did?" asks Dragonfly, turning around immediately, and laughing to himself. "I did not even notice."

He laughs again, and Butterfly joins him in the lighthearted laughter as a scent fills the air, a scent Butterfly recognizes but cannot place; it is sweet and tickles at the senses. They round a slight bend in the river, and just off the bank is a grove of trees with golden fruits the color of the rising and setting sun, the very source of the scent becoming intoxicating as they fly nearer; and Butterfly finds herself fluttering toward them without even choosing to do so.

"What are those?" asks Dragonfly loudly and excitedly.

"Fruit and nectar," says Butterfly; "and where there is fruit, there are bound to be aphids and all manner of things for you to hunt and eat as you do."

"They smell delicious!" says Dragonfly, speeding toward the grove and dashing among the branches, swooping into swarms of tiny, unsuspecting insectoid prey for him to eat.

Butterfly winces for a moment at the thought and sight and then shrugs it off and laughs as she settles upon one of the fruits that had fallen to the ground and is split open, revealing its nectar and pulp inside for her to suckle and drink.

There are many of the fallen golden orbs among the ground, surrounded by all manner of flora and fauna. Butterfly and Dragonfly drift from one to the next, feeling quite relaxed and giddy, their flights from one fruit to the next becoming staggering and even a collision or two is made, resulting in their hysterical laughter as they move on to the next fruit.

"What is this sensation?" asks Dragonfly, his speech slower than his normal hyper speed.

"I have no idea," says Butterfly, her speech even slower, her laughter even louder; "but I can't stop laughing."

A gust of wind surprises Butterfly and sends her upward, not far, but enough to startle her as she glides back down to the fruit she had been drinking from.

"Hey!" she shouts.

"What happened?" asks Dragonfly, having not seen Butterfly suddenly burst into the air.

Another gust of wind comes from the other direction and sends Butterfly in the air again.

"Hey," she shouts, her agitation growing to near fury. "Stop that!"

"I didn't do it!" slurs Dragonfly. "At least I don't think I did," he whispers to himself, suddenly unsure of exactly what it is he is doing.

Butterfly lands back upon the fruit, and the gust of wind comes again even stronger from the other direction and sends her sprawling toward Dragonfly; she smashes right into him, sending them falling into the opening of the sticky fruit.

"Yeah, that definitely was not me," mutters Dragonfly as he climbs out of the fruit and begins wiping the sticky nectar off his wings.

"It's the Wind!" shouts Butterfly, excited, confused, and doing her best to flutter her wings, but the heavy nectar keeps her grounded.

A loud laughter bursts out into the air coming from the bushel of flowers directly in front of them, and out rolls a hare in a fit of hysterics, doubled over and gripping its stomach in pure delight.

"It was you!" shouts Butterfly.

In her exclamations, she leans too far back over the edge of the fruit and falls right back into the opening, back into the sticky nectar, sending the hare into an even greater roar of laughter, infecting Dragonfly as he joins in on the joyousness.

Butterfly emerges from inside the fruit and flicks her wing as hard as she can at Dragonfly, sending a splash of the sticky nectar right into his face, making him stumble and tip over right off the edge of the fruit and onto the ground below; and now all three are in full hysterics.

"A grand trick, Uncle Hare!" says Dragonfly as he climbs back onto the fruit with Butterfly.

The hare rolls off its back and sits on its rear haunches, picking up one of the nearby fruits and draining its nectar into its open mouth.

"Thank you, Dragonfly," says the hare, taking a bite out of the fruit. "I thought so too."

"Some trick," says Butterfly, louder than she intended; "now our wings are stuck, and we cannot fly."

Dragonfly sputters his wings and realizes she is correct; they are too sticky, and he cannot lift off the ground; though, now, he does not seem to mind as much as he normally would have in such a predicament. He is too busy eyeing the nectar of the fruit he is sitting upon.

"What is the rush?" asks Uncle Hare with a grin, taking another bite of the fruit. "Have you got somewhere to be in a hurry?"

"We're going to the end of the river," says Butterfly with a sharp snap.

"The end?" asks Uncle Hare, with a belch and chuckle. "Don't be so quick to get to the end that you miss all the wonders of the journey there."

"We're not rushing!" says Butterfly, feeling herself reacting to Uncle Hare's words, without pause, and with an agitation she cannot explain, adding an air of false assuredness to her words she knows will be seen through as soon as she speaks, but unable to stop. "We just know where we're going."

"Oh, oh, is that so?" asks Uncle Hare. "Then you saw the open meadow with rolling green fields and the lagoon of the three waterfalls whose mists turn the waters there a flowery pink, with the old cherry blossom tree dipping into the surface waters, lilies and lotuses floating atop the mirrored waters. A most beautiful sight and sacred place; you must not have missed it. It is there just before the bend you followed to get here."

Uncle Hare looks on at Butterfly and tosses the drained fruit over his shoulder, looking around at the ground, picking up another one, and tipping its nectar into his mouth with another grin.

"I didn't see any—" stammers Butterfly, turning back toward the riverbank and the direction they had come. "Dragonfly, did you—?"

"Did I what?" asks Dragonfly, the words more falling out of his mouth than are spoken, as he looks up at Butterfly from the fruit he is drinking, belches, and hiccups loudly as Butterfly rolls her eyes and turns her glare back on Uncle Hare.

"Don't fret," says Uncle Hare with a chuckle and shrug. "When your wings dry, you can go back and look for yourself, if you wish."

Butterfly shakes her wings and then watches as Dragonfly slowly slides down the side of the fruit and comes to rest on the ground, not moving.

"I think I've had enough to drink," says Dragonfly in a whisper, with another belch, eliciting another chuckle from Uncle Hare.

"How long will we be stuck like this?" asks Butterfly, shaking her wings again and looking at Uncle Hare.

Uncle Hare tosses the drained fruit over his shoulder and picks up yet another one, tossing it up in the air a couple times before lounging back in the grass.

"Don't worry," he says, taking a gentle sip of the fruit's nectar. "Not forever. About as long as it will take me to tell you this story,"

"Story?" asks Dragonfly in a mumbling voice of slurred speech. "What story? I like stories."

"The story of how the sun was conquered," says Uncle Hare, sitting up, taking another sip of the fruit's nectar, and setting it down beside him. He rubs his paws together and raises them up to the sky in the direction of the sun, blocking out its light in front of him.

Dragonfly remains leaning up against the fruit, unmoving; and Butterfly drifts down to rest upon a blade of grass directly in front of Uncle Hare, who lowers his paws and leans forward over his haunches.

"One day, the hare-god was fast asleep in the valley," says Uncle Hare. "The Sun decided to mischievously burn his back, causing the hare-god to leap up with a great howl.

'You there, I knew it was you, playing this trick on me!' he yelled up at the Sun. 'I will show you what it is to feel the heat, watch me now!'

And so, the hare-god took off and set out to fight the Sun. On the way he stopped to pick and roast some vegetables for himself. When the planters of the vegetables ran out and tried to punish him for thieving, he scratched a hole into the ground and ran in, out of sight.

His pursuers shot arrows and threw rocks into the hole, but the hare-god had his magic breath with him, and it was an awfully strong breath, for with it he turned all the arrows and stones aside.

'The thief is in here,' said one of the pursuers.

'Let us get to him from this side,' said the other.

So, they acquired flints and shovels, and they began to dig.

'That's how it's going to be, is it?' said the hare-god. 'I know a way out of here that you don't.'

And with a few huffs and puffs of his breath and a few kicks of his hind legs, he reached a great fissure that led into the rock behind him, and there along this passage, he squeezed and scurried until he came to the edge in a niche. From here he could watch his enemies as they continued digging.

'Be buried in the grave you have dug for yourselves!' the hare-god shouted when the hole was exceptionally large, then he hurled down a magic ball and caved the earth in on their heads.

'To fight is as good fun as to eat,' said the hare-god, remarking to himself. 'Vengeance is my work. Everyone I meet will be an enemy. No one shall escape my wrath.'

And with that, the hare-god sounded his war whoop.

The next day of his journey to fight the Sun, the hare-god saw two men heating rocks and chipping arrowheads from them.

'Let me lend a hand,' said the hare-god, walking into their camp. 'Those hot rocks will not hurt me.'

'You would have us to believe you are a spirit, huh?' said the two men, laughing and jeering at the hare-god, whom they though only a mere hare.

'Not a ghost, but a better man than you,' answered the hare-god. 'Hold me over those hot rocks, and if I do not burn, then you must let me do the same to you.'

The two men did as the hare-god said, heating the rocks to redness in the fire, and they placed the hare-god against them but failed to see that by his magic breath he was keeping a current of air flowing between the hot surface of the stones and his body.

Rising, unscathed, the hare-god demanded that they also submit to the torture. And like brave warriors, they complied. When their flesh had been burned halfway through and they were dead, the hare-god sounded his war whoop and moved on.

In the morning of the third day of his journey to fight the Sun, the Wind brought words to the ears of the hare-god, words coming from some women atop a nearby cliff. They spoke of planning to kill him by rolling large boulders upon him as he passed. When he drew near, the hare-god pretended to eat something with such joy and delight that they asked him what it was that he was enjoying.

'Something oh-so sweet,' yelled the hare-god up to the women. 'Come to the cliff's edge, and I will throw some up to you.'

As they did, he threw something up into the air, so near to their reach that when they bent over and forward to seize it within their grasp, they crowded too close to the brink, lost their balance, fell over and off the cliff, and were killed.

'You are victims of your own greed,' said the hare-god as he looked upon them. 'One should never be so anxious as to kill oneself.'

This was all the hare-god had to say; he made no other comment, save sounding his war whoop, and he moved on.

On the fourth day of his journey to fight the Sun, the hare-god came upon two women making water jugs of willow baskets lined with black pitch, he heard one whispering to the other.

'Here comes that bad hare,' she said. 'How shall we destroy him?'

'What were you saying?' asked the hare-god politely as he came up to the women.

'We were just saying, here comes our grandson,' said the women with a smile.

'Oh, is that all?' replied the hare-god with a smile of his own. 'Then, please, let me get into one of these water jugs while you braid the neck.'

The hare-god jumped into the nearest one and lay still as they wove up the neck, then they laughed at the thought that it was braided too tight and small that the hare-god could never escape.

When suddenly the jug was shattered and exploded, and there stood the hare-god. The two women knew nothing of his magic breath.

'How did you get out?' they asked.

'Easily enough,' said the hare-god, standing above the remaining jug. 'These may hold water well enough, but they cannot hold men and women. Go ahead, try it, and see for yourself.'

They gave their consent, and the hare-god began weaving the neck of the water jug about them, and in a short while, he then had them caged.

'Now come on out," he called to them.

Try as they might, not a single willow branch could they bend or break.

'You are wise women, aren't you?' shouted the hare-god into the basket with a laugh. 'All bottled up in your own jugs! I am on my way to kill the Sun. In time, I shall learn how.'

Then as he sounded his war whoop, he struck them both dead with his magic ball and moved on.

On the fifth day of his journey to fight the Sun, the hare-god came upon the Bear and found him digging a hole to hide in, for he had heard of what the hare-god was doing and that he had been seen nearby.

'Do not be frightened, friend Bear," said the hare-god, speaking softly as he came up to the Bear. 'I am not the kind you need hide from. How could one such as me hurt so many people?'

Then the hare-god helped the Bear to dig his hole and den, and when it was finished, he went and hid behind a nearby rock. As the Bear thrust his head close, the hare-god launched his magic ball at the Bear's face and made an end of him.

The hare-god looked over the dead Bear and said aloud, 'I was afraid of this warrior,' said the hare-god as he looked over the dead Bear; 'but now he is dead in his den.'

He sounded his war whoop and moved on.

On the sixth day of his journey to fight the Sun, the hare-god met the tarantula, another clever trickster who had a club that would deal a fatal blow to others but could not and would not hurt himself.

The tarantula began to groan as the hare-god came close. He cried out that he was in pain from an evil spirit in his head, and the tarantula asked the hare-god to thump out the evil spirit. The hare-god nodded and said indeed he would. He plucked up the club in his hands and gave the Tarantula the soundest kind of a thwacking.

'Harder!' shouted the tarantula.

The hare-god then guessed that it was an enchanted weapon, and so he changed it for his magic ball, and he finished the tarantula in a single blow.

'That is a stroke of your own seeking,' said the hare-god, looking down at the dead tarantula. 'I am on my way to kill the Sun. Now I know that I can do it.'

He sounded his war whoop and moved on.

On the seventh day of his journey to fight the Sun, the hare-god came to the edge of the world and looked off into space, where thousands of careless peoples had fallen. There, the hare-god passed the night under a grand tree as he waited for the return of the Sun.

As dawn approached, the hare-god stood upon the brink of the earth and the instant the Sun appeared, he flung his magic ball with all his strength straight into the face of the Sun.

The surface of the Sun was broken into a thousand pieces that shattered and splayed all over the earth and kindled a tremendous conflagration.

The hare-god crept under the tree that had sheltered him, but it was no use against the increasing heat.

He attempted to run away as fast as he could, but the fire burned off all his toes, then both of his feet, and then both of his legs, and when the fire burned his body, he ran on his hands.

When his hands were burned off by the fire, he walked on the stumps of his arms. At last, only his head remained, and that went rolling down and over a hill into the valley, and it struck a rock.

When the hare-god's eyes finally burst and the tears gushed forth and moved on across the entire land, they put out the flames.

The Sun had been conquered and at his trial before the other gods, he was reprimanded for all his mischievous pranks and condemned thereafter to travel across the sky every day by the same path and trail. *

"Wait, who did the other gods reprimand?" asks Dragonfly, as curious as ever. "Was it the Sun? Or the hare-god?"

Butterfly was sure Dragonfly fell asleep, not noticing how enthralled to the story she, herself, was.

"How are those wings feeling now?" says Uncle Hare, chuckling, picking up the fruit he had set beside him, and taking a sip.

Both Butterfly and Dragonfly attempt to shake their wings and extend them, only to find they are stuck fast and will not move at all. No matter how hard they try, they will not budge or move.

Panic begins to set in, and then the roar of Uncle Hare's laughter startles them as they just look on in helpless bewilderment.

"Yeah, the sun will bake that nectar into glue on those delicate wings of yours," says Uncle Hare with a grin, taking another sip of the nectar.

Uncle Hare tosses the fruit over his shoulder as he springs into action, hopping here and there, grabbing a bit of grass from this, some weed of that, a bit of earthen dirt, a speck of mud, and without even a wince he pulls a tuft of his own fur from his cotton tail, smooshing it all together and then bounding, lightning quick, first to Butterfly, where he gently rubs the self-made salve throughout her wings and then over to Dragonfly where he does the same.

"Thank you, Uncle," says Dragonfly and Butterfly, together, unfurling and fluttering their wings as they lift into the air.

"Don't mention it,' says Uncle Hare with a wink.

"Is there really such a meadow and lagoon as you say?" asks Butterfly as they begin to float back over toward the riverbank, away from the grove of golden fruits with their bewildering nectar. "Is it truly not far from here?"

"You'll have to go and see," Uncle Hare says with a grin at Butterfly. "Now, I must be moving on."

And with those final words, he bounds into the high grass and is unseen.

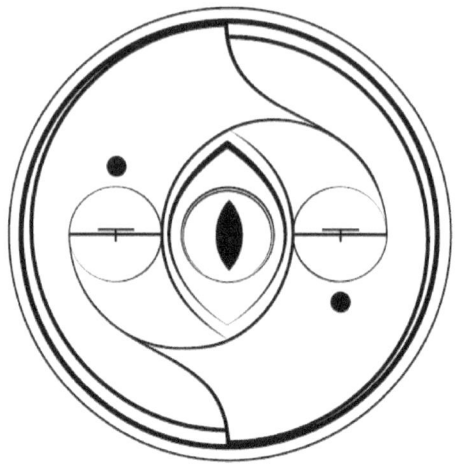

CHAPTER V

Auntie and the Queen of the Valley

B utterfly flaps her wings furiously, attempting to catch up to Dragonfly, who has already crossed the bank of the river, she flies farther from the grove of golden fruit trees with the setting sun at her back; she wants to tell Dragonfly of the waterfall lagoon and the meadow with rolling hills Uncle Hare had spoken of, to tell him they should go back and see if they had missed the sight of it.

Butterfly notices she is still moving sluggishly from the effects of the nectar she consumed, and it takes her longer than she would have liked before she finally flutters up next to Dragonfly, with the sun now nearly down below the horizon; the reflection of the moon can be seen sitting in the sky with the many hues of blues and purples. She lands upon a toadstool next to Dragonfly, while they look up at the colorful dusk sky, she forgets to remember to tell Dragonfly of the lagoon and meadow, and they sit there, enjoying the setting sun and rising moon.

One by one, a shining and shimmering twinkle begins to arrive in the sky. One after the other, and simultaneously, the stars begin to shine. Something else catches Butterfly's eye; at first, she thinks perhaps it is a cloud, and then she wonders if it is a falling star. She looks up, over, and there, descending from the trees above, lightly floating in descent, white and pure as a cloud, is a single feather. As it falls, its course means to land it directly between

Butterfly and Dragonfly.

The pair look at the feather and then at one another, and before either can speak a word, a large flash and streak of white swoops down directly in front of them, silent as could be until it speeds directly into the brush beneath the toadstool they had landed upon. The blur arises with a small serpent in its talons as the large, white, feathery creature spreads its enormous wings and ascends to a tree limb directly above Dragonfly and Butterfly. The serpent remains in its talons, dead and hanging over the branch, swaying gently back and forth.

Dragonfly and Butterfly look up at the creature, enormous and all white with a flattened face and two enormous golden eyes that are peering directly at them. Butterfly feels her heartbeat rising, and she attempts the irregular-to-regular breathing rhythm, but the fear holds as she looks upon the great white, feathery beast with the dead serpent in its claws. She feels just as immobile as she did when held in Grandmother Spider's webbing, though this time, there is no web. Only the feeling of being stuck, frozen, and helpless; and even though there is nothing physically holding her in place, she cannot move.

An entirely new sense of shock snaps her out of her immobility, and she feels herself regaining control over her senses, body, limbs, and wings. She blinks as she watches what she nearly cannot believe is happening. Dragonfly is flying up toward the great feathered beast. He stops directly at the head of the serpent and pauses to look at it and then floats up directly before the great white and feathered creature.

"Thank you, Auntie Owl," he says. "Surely the serpent meant to surprise us and make of us its supper."

Auntie Owl blinks slowly and cocks her head.

"Had his last already, it seems," says Auntie Owl. "Supper that is."

The large white bird Dragonfly refers to as Auntie Owl gives a delicate chuckle which Dragonfly echoes and is so light it brings a flutter to Butterfly's wings as she finds herself moving up toward where Dragonfly and the one he calls Auntie Owl are sharing the gentle laugh.

She lands upon the tree near, but not too near, Dragonfly and Auntie Owl.

"Yes, thank you...Auntie," says Butterfly. "We owe you our lives."

"Take care with saying such things, Butterfly," says Auntie Owl in a soft and echoing sing-song voice, slowly turning her head to face Butterfly. "There are those who will hold you to such an oath. As for me, you owe no such thing as grand as your life. It may remain yours."

"But we do owe you something other than our thanks?" asks Butterfly, catching on to the meaning within Auntie Owl's words.

"Well," says Auntie Owl with a gently laugh, "I do believe that my flying all the way here from the north, at the request of the Wind, to be the herald of the news that winter draws near and saving you two delicate things from the jaws of this sneaky serpent grants me a little more compensation than a thank-you. Wouldn't you agree?"

"That depends," says Butterfly without returning Auntie Owls laughter.

Auntie Owl blinks and laughs even louder but still as sweetly and lightly as a song in the wind that makes Butterfly both relax and feel anxious at the same time.

"The Wind spoke to you?" asks Dragonfly as he hovers closer, dangerously close to Auntie Owl's beak, thinks Butterfly.

"Of course," says Auntie Owl, looking at Dragonfly with a curious tilt of her head. "I was asked to bring news that winter fast approaches the green forest. You should not winter here; it will be much too cold and barren for many days and nights."

"Where should we go?" asks Dragonfly. "First, we must find the Wind."

"Then seek the Wind," says Auntie Owl, keeping her amber-gold eyes on Dragonfly. "Perhaps the Wind will tell you where you shall weather the coming winter storms."

"Now about that compensation," says Auntie Owl, turning back toward Butterfly.

Butterfly returns Auntie Owl's gaze and feels a strange sense of confidence that she realizes makes no logical sense, as Auntie Owl can easily devour her at any moment she wishes; still, she feels defiant.

"Is our appreciation and gratitude not enough compensation?" she asks.

"Two words of appreciation for two lives saved," says Auntie Owl, showing no signs of taking offense to Butterfly. "Yes, that is enough. However, for my long, arduous, and lonely journey to here from the north and for the return journey, I have nothing to show for it. Not even a new friend have I made, for all that I speak to will not return with me, and they are saddened by the truth of the news of change I must bring."

Auntie Owl's words speak to Butterfly's heart, and she knows of the loneliness that the Owl speaks of, but still there remains a tide of suspicion within her, and she attempts to find the words to properly speak and convey this when she notices Auntie Owl's head tilting at a harsh angle, and her amber eyes peering at her.

"You still do not trust me," says Auntie Owl. "For why? After I saved your life, when easily I could have taken both of you and the serpent for my own supper."

Butterfly shudders at being seen so clearly without speaking the words in her thoughts.

"I do not trust you, that is true," she says softly and apologetically but with conviction.

"Well, as my kind is known to eat yours, I cannot say I blame you or would call you a fool for your suspicion," says Auntie Owl, blinking slowly. "Though I have made no move to do any such thing."

"I have known another owl before who did not devour," says Butterfly. "This one lied and said change was wrong and to stay away from it. To only remain the same. If I had listened, never would I have become Butterfly."

"I see," says Auntie Owl, nodding and humming within a slight pause. "Yes. We owls are known for our wise words, our wisdom; although, this too, may become a pitfall—a trap—for when one believes they truly know a thing, that is the moment they stop learning. When Belief becomes the death of Knowledge. Even us masters must ever remain students."

Butterfly relaxes at Auntie Owl's words but cannot find her own to respond and continue the thread of conversation.

"What is the compensation you seek, then, Auntie Owl?" she asks instead.

Auntie Owl slowly stretches out her massive wings from her body, the beautiful feathers flexing outward and then folding in on themselves as she tucks them back close to her body, turning her head from Butterfly to Dragonfly and back again.

"An equal exchange is all," she says. "Stay here, this night, with me in this tree and share with me company and a story. I shall keep you from harm while you sleep, and you shall keep the loneliness away from me for a time. Indeed, it has been an age since I have had anyone to speak with who was not so disheartened by the news of change I bring that they could not bear to look upon me."

Butterfly and Dragonfly eagerly consent give their consent with a nod, a nod which Auntie Returns with a flapping of her wings and fluffing of her great white feathers.

"Long ago," says Auntie Owl; "an exceedingly long time ago now, I travelled far south, delivering and heralding the same news of change I carry with me now, on this day.

In my travels, I crossed a most fertile land of green and blue, and more abundant than any of the other lands I had been in, over, or across.

There were many plant people, animal people of all legs, the crawlers and the feathered, even the two-legged; and it is of the two-legged of this land this story speaks.

In this most lavish valley, there were natural springs of crystal water and an enormous lake that filled the lowest point of the land. There were warm and cool spring pools here and there with meadows, grottos, glades, and all manner of vegetation, such as corn, beans, squash, sunflowers, and groves of trees cultivating seed pods.

There remained a strong connection between the entire valley and the two-legged peoples who dwelled there.

In the early days of this valley, the people there were ruled by a queen. A most beautiful queen, she was; though, the queen was entirely vain.

She was demanding and commanded the people to build a palace for her that would be grander and more beautiful than anything that her neighbors of the four directions had ever seen or built, especially her southern neighbors, named the *Aztecs*.

She ordered all her people to begin construction of this most beautiful palace and forced them to transport heavy amounts of marble, stone, quartz, and timber to the site where the palace was to be built.

The people considered it their duty to make the queen's dreams come true without complaint, for royalty was sacred. They worked exceedingly hard to please her and dragged and hauled the massive stones and logs of timber over long and great distances.

As many years passed, a fear began to overtake the queen. The fear that she would die long before the magnificent palace was completed; and so, she became even more demanding and commanded her people to build faster.

She even insisted and commanded her own family to work alongside the rest of the people to build her the palace of her dreams.

Gradually, without realization, the people became slaves to the queen. Even her family. The queen began to lash their backs if they slowed in their work, even during the high noon heat of the sun; she would whip and strike their naked backs.

It was during one of these floggings that the queen whipped the back of her own daughter, yelling at the young girl that she was working too slowly.

Upon the first strike, the princess stopped working. She dropped the load of quartz she was carrying and turned to her mother. The princess cursed the queen, her mother, and her kingdom. At once, she fell to the ground, taken by heat and exhaustion, and there she died.

Then, in that immediate moment, the queen realized just how far her ultimate greed and obsession had taken her. She had destroyed her culture and replaced what was once rich in family values and love of nature and the land itself with not but slavery.

In her greed, she had thrown away the people and lifestyle she had loved most and who had genuinely loved her.

Sadly, her regret and insight were too late.

Soon after, all of nature and the land itself, the entire valley, began to turn on her. Punishing her for her wickedness, greed, lies, and shortsightedness. The sun increased its brightness and its heat, causing all the vegetation to whither and the green to turn brown until it blew away with the hot winds. The streams, springs, pools, and the great lake dried up and became not but cracks and crags in the hard earth; and the abundant animal peoples fled.

The once-fertile and beautiful green-and-blue valley was now a barren, dry, and extremely hot desert. Most of the queen's people died of starvation, and the ones that survived fled with the animals.

Only the queen and her nearly finished palace remained.

After all were gone and she was all that remained, the queen was struck with a grave illness.

With not a one to soothe or care for her or bring her medicine, she died alone in her empty and unfinished palace in the desert.

Legends say that glimpses of the half-finished palace may be seen, lifting into view, or as shifting mirages upon the horizon in the desert heat. That no two-legged people can cross that desert and yet live, that horses and other livestock will sink to their knees in wide drifts of dust; there is no water, and the heat is beyond devastating.

Animals that die in the valley, now desert, mummify but do not decay; and so, the bodies remain bleached across the sands and grassless plains.

On the eastern side of what is now called Dead Mountain are pointed white rocks that are said to be the ghosts of the people who died there because of the queen's greed and obsession. The once-beautiful valley was now called '*Ground Afire.*'

Never again did meadows of green grass grow in this desert, but many years after, a tribe of the two-legged people came to the desert, and for a thousand years, they lived and thrived there, constructing simple brush homes of dome-shaped desert dwellings that allowed breezes to come and go through arrow-weed walls.

Edible plants began to sprout, and cool springs filtered up through the ground here and there. Even wildlife slowly returned with the rains and water—big-horned sheep, rabbits, and lizards. A harvest season was aplenty with fruits, vegetables, and seeds. Pine nuts and beans were readily available.

The people made bows and arrows and hunted the desert and collected plants and made baskets that were so intricately coiled and woven that they could hold water without spill.

So, it came as a surprise to these two-legged people when one day, after generations of thriving within their desert home that had been so abundant and life-giving to and for them, there came a stranger who told them the tale of the history of their desert home and how to all other peoples it had come to be known as '*Death Valley*.'" *

Auntie Owl finishes the story and a few moments of silence pass.

"Where is this valley, Auntie Owl?" asks Dragonfly, interrupting the silence. "This desert?"

"It is both very far and very near," says Auntie Owl, looking at Dragonfly and then up into the night sky where the moon is now risen high.

"Will you cross over it when you return north?" asks Dragonfly.

"Yes," says Auntie Owl, now peering down from the moon at Dragonfly.

"Can we go there too?" Dragonfly asks curiously.

"Not today," Auntie Owl says with a gentle and light laugh.

"Dragonfly, do not forget our journey upon the river to find it's ending and our meeting with the Wind," Butterfly says to Dragonfly with a tinge of anxiousness in her voice.

"I haven't, and I am not," says Dragonfly. "I was only curious where it might be. I had never seen a forest, and now I have. There is still much I have not seen, including green valleys and hot deserts."

"Don't fret," says Auntie Owl, chuckling lightly. "You will see much, still, young Dragonfly."

Auntie Owl bends down and picks up the serpent she has clutched in her talons with her beak and devours it. She ruffles her feathers and spreads her wings out wide.

"Now, stay here upon the limb," she says. "I will be around and near. My senses are alive with the night, and I shall guard and protect you from any danger that may come near. Rest through the night, and in the morning, continue your journey to the river's end and where, there, you will find the Wind. We shall meet again, without question."

Dragonfly and Butterfly watch Auntie Owl swoop from the branch, and the moonlight shines and reflects off her pure white feathers, creating a glowing aura of light around her as she moves into the shadows of the forest, beyond where their eyes can follow.

Butterfly and Dragonfly remain there, blinking into the darkness of the night, quietly listening, and without noticing, they drift off into slumber.

The next moment they are aware of, the night has given way to a gentle glow of the sun just beginning to peek over the horizon, bringing the dawn of a new morning.

They stretch out their wings as Auntie Owl had done, and down the tree they go, rejoining the river on their journey to its destination.

INTERMISSION

"How are you enjoying the brew, Traveler?"

"Yes, the tea. Good, isn't it? I gathered, dried, and brewed the leaves myself. I like my teas dark, robust, and earthen. The trick to brewing tea is all in patience and the time, Traveler.

You see, if you remove the tea from the heat too soon, some impurities will remain, and the tea will be contaminated. Still useful and drinkable, but not as good or beneficial as it could have been and at times, even a little dangerous to one's wellbeing.

If you leave the tea in the heat too long, it will be entirely useless and undrinkable, and you will have to start all over again from the beginning. See, Traveler, it is all about the timing."

"Hm? The fire? What do you want to know about—oh you cad! Did I make the fire myself too, you ask? Ha! Your cleverness abounds again, Traveler. To answer your question—yes and no.

I dug the pit with my hands, I quarried, carried, and placed the stones, I gathered the kindling and made the tinder, I struck Materia against Materia and sparks erupted from which the fire was ignited into life; but no, I did not create the fire. I created the space for the fire to be and as you can now see, Traveler, here the fire is being."

"Oh! Say, Traveler, you've reminded me of a story! Stop me if you've heard this one before—don't actually stop me, that's a figure of speech, Traveler. Never interrupt a storyteller telling a story, it ruins the enchantment.

Now how did it go, let me think, just a moment—Ah! Yes, that's it, thank you, fire!

There is a Daoist Master that says, 'Imagine you set out upon a path of cultivation and enlightenment. Along your path you come upon the Devil in the road who calls out to you, slighting you. You stop and argue with the Devil. And now the Devil has won.'

Have you heard this story before, Traveler?"

"Hmm. Curious and interesting. Well, then, I offer you this suggestion: If, or when, the Devil does happen to appear upon your path, instead of arguing and engaging, take the moment to sit and forget the slight, forget the argument and forget the judgement of the Devil. Sit and ask a simple question; and invite the Devil to join you for tea.

Brewing and drinking tea is an ancient process of alchemy, Traveler, an agent of change—both inner and outer.

You see, I have two cups of tea. I offer one to the Devil and pour one for myself. I fill the cups with tea, and we share a moment of stillness. We enjoy the tea and learn what may be learned. When the cups are empty, there is the realization that there are not two cups of tea; and then stand and continue the way.

Now, Traveler, let us sit and enjoy our tea together, from the Calcination to the Crystallization, and we will reveal what there is to reveal."

CHAPTER VI

Friends and Strangers

The morning is crisp with a chill in the air as Butterfly and Dragonfly make their way down the river. The waters have become still, their movement and flow barely noticeable; and the riverbed is now visible beneath the surface. The sun has not risen completely over the horizon yet, turning the sky and clouds many shades of purples, pinks, and oranges as they continue, enjoying the stillness and quiet of the morning.

A strange sound of echoing neighs breaks through the silence, coming from ahead where the river seems to almost disappear as tall reeds cross its surface from one bank to the other. Butterfly and Dragonfly fly over the reeds, and here the river opens wide. Large boulders and flat ground extend far out and wide, and there are pools here and there and small cascading waterfalls; down over a short cliff's edge, the water moves down into a turning foam. The river continues after, flowing full and deep once again.

It is here among the widened plateau that the echoed neighs are emitting, for here, Butterfly and Dragonfly come upon the sight of two of the most enormous horses who have ever been seen or spoken of by any, save for those who have seen them. One of them is all black. Black as the night, not a spot or shine of any color from mane to hoof, and the other is all white, as pure as had been Auntie Owl's feathers, perhaps even more so, as not a single mark or brand of color can be found or seen. As Butterfly and Dragonfly draw closer to the enormous horses, who are encircling each other, they notice they are mistaken in their first summary of the horses' coloring. There, upon the middle of the forehead of the black horse, is a small white spot, barely visible until you stand before him; and there, upon the white horse, is a small black spot in the same place upon the forehead.

The two horses circle one another, whinnying and neighing, splashing through the shallow pools, raising on hind legs, clashing hoofs, and then circling one another again and again. Butterfly and Dragonfly cannot be sure if they are laughing, playing, arguing, fighting, or conversing. They have no idea what is transpiring between these two enormous equestrian creatures they have come upon.

They sit upon two tall reeds, as close as they dare, and they watch the black-and-white horses continue to circle one another atop the river plateau of pools and falls.

Gradually, as if they are suddenly within earshot, even though they have not moved, Butterfly and Dragonfly begin to understand what the two horses are saying to one another.

"The medicine man was sitting on a boulder by the old path when a horse and rider came galloping quickly," says the black horse. "It appears the rider had somewhere important to go."

The horses rear up together and come splashing down, continuing to encircle one another.

"And so, the medicine man stood atop his boulder and shouted at the rider as he came nearer, 'Where are you going?'" says the white horse. "As the horse and rider sped by the medicine man, the rider shouted back, 'I don't know—ask the horse!'" *

The great horses rear up again, clashing their hooves together and braying in laughter as they come crashing down into the shallow water and resume their circling trot and gallop.

Dragonfly looks at Butterfly and quickly dashes from one reed to another, closer to the horses as they continue their circle dance. Butterfly, too mesmerized by their movement and way, flutters closer to a crop of tall reeds with Dragonfly, and they listen to the black-and-white horses speak in their strange way.

"There once was a teacher of warriors with two pupils, one male and one female," says the black horse. "The teacher did not call his pupils by name but instead called them both Meta."

The horses pick up speed in their circled galloping, water splashing up and creating a rainbow spectrum of color in the mist around them.

"The teacher was training the two young warriors about balance, and each day they were to perform a task to earn their daily meal," says the black horse. "For their task, one pupil would balance a tall spear atop their head while the other slowly climbed to the top. Once at the top, the pupil would remain there, while the other walked slowly along the ground. The two pupils had to maintain complete focus and balance to prevent any injury and earn their daily meal."

The horses rear up and clash their hooves together before crashing down into the water and now galloping even faster than before, sending water spraying above and around them, high above their tall backs.

"One day," says the white horse. "The teacher said to the pupils, 'Meta! You will watch out for the other while the other watches out for you. That way you can help maintain concentration and balance and prevent an accident so you may earn your daily meal.'

The pupils were wise warriors, and they said to their teacher, 'Dear Teacher, I think it would be better for both to look after oneself. To look after oneself means to look after both of us. That way we will prevent any accident, and we will surely earn our daily meal.'"

*

The two great horses rear up again from opposite sides of the circle they are creating in their galloping. So fast do they stop and rear that the water splashes up, over, and in front of them in a wide arch. They crash down to the ground, shaking their manes and whinnying and neighing with laughter before beginning their circling again.

As the two great horses begin slowly trotting in their circling motion around one another, Butterfly watches Dragonfly cautiously make his way toward them, hovering slowly instead of his usual quick dashing and darting.

Dragonfly is now as near to them as they are to each other.

"Hello, great horse friends," says Dragonfly, shouting over the trampling of giant hooves in the shallow water. "I am Dragonfly."

The two horses do not stop circling, and they do not speak, but they do turn and face Dragonfly. With their eyes upon him, they keep circling, widening their circle until Dragonfly is now in the middle of them, and they continue their circle gallop around him. Without speaking a word, the great horses stop, turn, and begin circling around Dragonfly in the opposite direction of which they have been traveling.

"With all respect," says Dragonfly; "I am curious where these stories you speak of are from?"

The horses both throw up their heads and whinny and then place their eyes back on Dragonfly.

"There once was a chief of the Nation known as hero and leader by the two-legged people," says the black horse. "He held fame, power, wealth, humility, and devotion."

"Often did the chief visit with the tribe's medicine man to learn, says the white horse. "They got along very well, and it did not matter that he was chief. Their relationship was of teacher and student. The medicine man, the revered teacher, and the chief, the respectful student."

"One day," says the black horse; "the chief asked the medicine man, 'Revered Teacher, what is it that we call Ego?'

The medicine man's face turned red, and in a condescending and insulting tone, he shouted at the chief, 'What kind of stupid question is that?'"

"The chief was so shocked and surprised by the medicine man's unexpected response that he became very sullen and angry," says the white horse. "Seeing the chief's anger, the medicine man smiled and said, 'That, Great Chief, is Ego.'" *

The horses slow their trotting to a near stall, taking a single slow step one after another as they keep their eyes upon Dragonfly, who stays hovering in the same spot, listening as they speak in their strange alternating way.

"If you throw a fist of spices into a cup of water, the water will be undrinkable," says the black horse.

The two great horses stop, turn, and begin circling again in the opposite direction at the same slow pace.

"If you throw a fist of spices into the river, the people can still draw water to cook, wash, and drink," says the white horse.

"The river is immense and has the capacity to receive, embrace, and transform," says the black horse.

The horses stop, turn, and continue their slow-paced circle back in the other direction. Dragonfly remains hovering in the center.

"When hearts become small," says the white horse; "understanding and compassion are limited, and there is suffering. Others are then not tolerated or accepted of their shortcomings and are demanded and commanded to change."

"But when hearts are expanded," says the black horse; "those same things cannot cause suffering anymore. Then there is much understanding and compassion and the embrace of others. Then others are accepted as they are."

"And then they have a chance to transform," * says the white horse.

The two great horses shake their heads and manes and whinny and then stop, turn, and continue their circle walk, even slower than before, seeming to take an entire breath between steps.

Butterfly is frightened, curious, and intrigued as she watches the enormous horses surrounding Dragonfly. She looks on and listens to them continue their strange way of speech as they look directly at him.

"The ways of disposing of the dead are many," says the black horse in a low and deep tone. "Some corpses are placed in the ground. Some corpses are put in trees. Some are mummified and preserved. Some are burned and cremated. Some are forgotten. Some are even mutilated."

The two great horses stop, turn, and continue their step-by-step walk in a circle around Dragonfly, never breaking an unblinking eye as they continue speaking in their strange way.

"When a warrior dies," says the white horse; "the warrior is buried on the western side of the camp so that the soul may follow the setting sun into the spirit world. The warrior's bow, arrows, and valuables are buried with the warrior, and the warrior's most trusted pony is killed at the grave of the warrior so that the warrior may appear among their tribe in the happy hunting grounds, mounted and equipped."

The two great horses stop, turn, and continue their slow-stepping circle around Dragonfly, still unblinking and without breaking eye contact. Dragonfly continues to hover in the center, following each great horse as it takes its turn to speak, and he listens to their words.

"Once there was an old warrior who died," says the black horse. "The old warrior was without relatives and was poor. So, the tribe thought that any kind of a horse would do for the warrior to range upon the fields of paradise and the happy hunting grounds. The tribe killed a spavined old mare and left the grave."

"Days later," says the white horse; "the recently passed and unlamented came galloping into the tribe's camp on the back of a gangly, tailless, emaciated, rib-cage-showing horse, calling for dinner. The unlamented was formally presented a piece of meat at the end of a long pole. Securing the meat, the unlamented offered themselves to the eyes of the tribe. The people were alarmed and frightened by the sight of the old warrior's glaring eyes and sunken cheeks."

The horses stop, turn, and continue their slow circle in the same, unblinking way, not breaking stride.

"The old, unlamented warrior tells the tribe that they have come back to haunt them for being a stingy and inconsiderate lot," says the black horse. "For the gatekeeper of heaven had refused the old warrior admittance on such an ill-conditioned mount. The tribe broke their camp, immediately, in panic and dismay. To this day, the people of that tribe have sacrificed only the best horses whenever an unfriended one journeys into the spirit world."*

The two great horses stop circling, they look at Dragonfly for a long breath of a moment and then begin walking toward him from opposing directions; where before they seemed to walk only in a circling motion, now they walk directly toward one another, step after step. Dragonfly hovers just above the height of their enormous back, at level with their wide-opened eyes.

Butterfly watches on in hushed silence as the two great horses arrive directly in front of one another, next to Dragonfly. The two great horses lean their large heads forward and touch foreheads upon the small black-and-white spots that rest there.

With their foreheads pressed together, they begin moving their hind legs around, circling outward. Dragonfly spins directly above them slowly.

The two great horses pick up speed, separating their heads and begin widening the circle, from walk, to trot, to gallop, to all-out run as the circle widens and widens, the water splashing high above the enormous creatures as Dragonfly continues to spin higher and higher.

The thundering of the great horses' hooves begins to shake the ground, rocks and pebbles tumble over into the river, and the black horse and the white horse break off in different directions, one going over and across one side of the bank and the other going over and across the other side.

Dragonfly hovers back to the reed that Butterfly is still resting upon, and they watch the two great horses as they run in great and fast strides across the land, into the deep forest and out of view.

CHAPTER VII

Love and Strawberries

As Dragonfly and Butterfly remain upon the reeds, they are unaware that they are swaying back and forth, gently at first, as they watch the two great horses gallop away into the forest on opposite sides of the riverbank.

Their enormous hooves are shaking the ground and reverberating off the trees so tremendously loud that it seems as though the sound is emanating from the very sky.

Awareness of the swaying of the reeds is awakened within both Dragonfly and Butterfly at the same instant.

"The Wind?" they ask in unison, turning to one another with widened eyes.

A large gust sends the reeds swaying halfway to the ground as another awareness awakens within the two that sends a chill throughout their bodies. The sound of the great horses' hooves has not dissipated, though they are many moments from sight now. The sound is, indeed, coming from the sky above.

Dragonfly and Butterfly look to the sky that is now rolling with gray and blackened clouds, hiding the sun from view, and with a loud *krack-ka-boom*, thunder rolls and rumbles across the sky, and drops of rain begin to descend from the moving clouds.

"Not wind," says Dragonfly over the rumbling thunder; "storm."

The two take off from the reeds together and fly across the shallow plateau of the river, the gusts of speechless winds picking up speed and carrying them along more than they are propelling themselves. Down the shallow waterfalls they go, the rain fall becoming a steady downpour instead of a light drizzle, and another deep rumbling of thunder echoes from up above.

"We need shelter, Dragonfly," shouts Butterfly.

The river deepens beneath them as they move away from the cascading falls of the plateau of the great horses, waves of white water cresting in rapid succession as they speed along through the wind and rain, another rumbling of thunder, deep and building.

Ahead of the two, the river becomes divided, a fork in the water separated by an enormous tree whose roots extend into the boulders and the river itself.

"Which way?" asks Butterfly, who can barely flap her wings as the rain and wind seem more in control of her movements and direction.

Dragonfly is looking up at the nearly pitch-black cloud that is funneling above them when the loudest *KRACK-KA-BOOM* crashes from the clouds, and light from within the blackness erupts from its center in tendrils, colliding into a single streak and bolt that flashes from the dark cloud to the gigantic tree right in front of them, setting it immediately ablaze at the base of its trunk.

The thunder jolts and frightens both Dragonfly and Butterfly enough to make them halt in their flight. Dragonfly hovers there, mesmerized by the climbing flames that have become an entire inferno. Rising from the base, up the trunk, and into the dry autumn branches, the entire tree is immediately aflame, and Dragonfly cannot take his eyes away from the beauty of its light and warmth.

"Dragonfly!" shouts Butterfly, fluttering frantically. "Dragonfly! We must move!"

She calls and yells, again and again, as Dragonfly just hovers there, completely enthralled by the flickering flames of the emblazoned tree before them.

Butterfly flies directly in front of his face, hoping to break his eye contact from the fire; the tree crackles and bursts forth embers as the trunk of the tree cracks and splits directly up the center, cleaving it in two. Thousands of specks of light and ember rush from the splitting tree and one tiniest little speck of flame reaches out and lands upon Butterfly's wing.

The sound of the Butterfly's scream of pain rocks Dragonfly from his infernal reverie, and his sight is filled with the image of Butterfly falling through the air, a whisp of flame upon her left wing.

"Butterfly!" yells Dragonfly.

He dashes forward to grab her but misses, and, seemingly in slow motion, they meet one another's gaze before Butterfly plummets into the waters of the river below, the tiniest hint of steam arising from its surface as it extinguishes the flame that was upon her wing while she sinks beneath the surface of the turning white waters.

Unable to say a word, Dragonfly flies down with all his might to where Butterfly vanished beneath the waters. He searches and darts and dashes from here to there along the water's surface, evading both cresting waves and swells and the floating fire embers from the still-burning tree that are increasingly filling the air around him.

One of the embers sizzles across his scales, and he feels the burning sensation. He dips and rolls around another and another. There are too many. He cannot stay here and not be completely consumed by the flames. He makes a choice and zips through the torrent of flaming specks of ash and cinder.

Thunder crashes overhead again, rolling through the sky as Dragonfly speeds down the river, his eyes darting frantically in front of him to avoid the floating embers and down below, still searching for signs of Butterfly.

Another narrow miss and a sizzling hiss and burn from a scrape of one of the embers as he maneuvers by. Too close to the water's surface, the white water splashes up and dampens his wings, slowing him down.

Thunder crashes again, *KRACK-KA-BOOM*, accompanied by another lightning bolt striking the ground off the riverbank, this one sending Dragonfly spinning and tumbling forward and down, smacking into a rock in the river.

He lies there, the rain falling upon him, the orange-and-yellow and black-and-gray floating forms of ember and ash floating like tiny fireflies above him.

The sounds of the burning tree, the wind whistling through grass, reed, and leaves, and the rushing water around him, with the thunder still rumbling across the sky. He thinks of Butterfly as darkness overtakes him.

From within the total darkness, a light begins to shine. Without even opening his eyes, Dragonfly knows he is awake. The light is warm and brightening; it is moving, almost dancing. He nearly fears to open his eyes and bring life to the awareness he dares not speak aloud.

Dragonfly opens his eyes slowly. The clouds above are still gray, though not black, and they are moving quickly across the sky, rays of sunlight showing through them here and there, sending shimmering glimmers of light dancing and bounding across the river that has once again calmed to its natural flow state. The once-blazing tree is now smoking and aglow but no longer enflamed.

As Dragonfly's eyes adjust to the sights around him, another image comes into view that was not there before. A face. A smiling and curious face with large eyes and a slick and slender body of red, orange, and deep brown, with four legs and a tail that is half serpent and half finned. The image then opens its mouth wide, and Dragonfly readies himself to surrender to death.

"Hello," says the wide-opened mouth.

"Hello," Dragonfly says without moving, still stunned and ready to die.

"Are you not frightened?" asks the reddish, wide-mouthed creature as it cocks it head.

"Why would I be frightened?" asks Dragonfly, stretching his wings.

"Well, I intended to eat you," says the creature, cocking its head to the other side; "if you hadn't noticed."

"Oh," says Dragonfly, turning to look at the creature in its solid black eyes. "Why haven't you?"

The creature pauses and looks Dragonfly head to tail.

"Because you seem incredibly sad," it says; "and I do not eat sad things. I do not want to become sad."

"I appreciate that," says Dragonfly, raising his customary one eye and lowering the other. "Thank you."

The creature seems to think a moment as it looks up to the sky and then back to Dragonfly.

"You're welcome," it says. "Perhaps I will make you happy and then eat you. And then we will both be happy, eh?"

Dragonfly pauses and stares at the creature who blinks one eye and then the other. Dragonfly cannot help himself and just begins laughing.

The creature stamps its feet and smiles.

"It's a deal, then!" it says. "What would make you happiest?"

Dragonfly stops laughing and looks down at the flat but moving waters of the surface of the river.

"To find my friend," he says.

The creature looks around, left and right, up, and down, and then back to Dragonfly.

"Who is your friend?" it asks.

"Butterfly," says Dragonfly in a hoarse whisper, the painful burning sensations throughout his body awakening at the sound of her name.

The creature stamps its feet again and turns in a quick circle.

"Excellent," says the creature. "I know where to find the butterflies. Follow me!"

The creature moves to jump off the rock they are on, and into the river, but stops and turns to Dragonfly.

"How rude of me," it says; "I forgot introductions. I am Salamander. Pleased to meet you."

Dragonfly nods and cannot help but smirk and feel his heart flutter at daring to hope this Salamander might help him find his lost friend, Butterfly.

"Well met, Salamander," he says. "I am Dragonfly."

"Good, good, Dragonfly!" says Salamander with a great nod of its head. "Now follow, follow me!"

Salamander leaps off the rock into the river and, with a flick and swish of its tail, goes careening through the water as fast as Dragonfly flies.

Dragonfly dashes off in the wake of Salamander, hoping to hope.

"Where are we going?" asks Dragonfly, as Salamander rises to the surface with a gentle splash.

"Oh, this place has many names," says Salamander. "My favorite, I have heard it called 'Samanalakanda.' I like it because it almost sounds like my name!"

Salamander continues to splash over the surface of the water, his arms and legs tucked tight to his sides, to where it is difficult to distinguish him from fish or serpent.

"How long will it take us to get there?" asks Dragonfly, shouting down to Salamander as he continues following from just above the surface of the river.

Salamander descends below the surface for a moment and then returns.

"Not long," he says as he descends again and then returns. "I shall tell you a story I know to pass the time. Stay close and follow, follow me!"

Salamander, once again, descends beneath the surface and then returns. His swift movement now a steady rhythm and pace as they settle into a comfortable speed.

"When the world was all anew, among the two-legged people there was one man and one woman," says Salamander as Dragonfly does his best to listen and not keep thinking of Butterfly, and the memories of their separation. "They were happy for many sleeps and many seasons. Then they quarreled and had a battle.

After one such great battle, the woman left the man and began walking away from him to the east, toward the Sunland.

The man followed, for he felt sorry, but the woman walked straight on into the rising sun and would not look back at the man."

The flutter of a flapping wing catches Dragonfly's eye, and he looks to the surface of the river nearby. His heart nearly stops. He looks and realizes it is but a moth, sitting upon a leaf on the surface of the river, riding the current. Within the next moment, Salamander leaps from the water and catches the moth in its jaws and gulps it down as he then continues swimming on.

Dragonfly winces for a moment, and then his stomach makes a rumbling sound, and he laughs as he spots a swarm of gnats up ahead and begins his diving and rolling death dance to secure his own meal.

"After many more sleeps of traveling," says Salamander, as Dragonfly finishes the last of the river gnats. "The woman did not look back as she continued east, and the man followed behind, saddened and sorry. One day, the Sun came as the great Apportioner.

'Are you still angry with your wife?' the sun asked the man, feeling sorry for him.

'No,' said the man to the Sun.

The Sun smiled gently at the man.

'Would you like to have her come back to you?' asked the Sun.

'Yes,' the man said to the Sun.

And so, the Sun made a great big patch of huckleberries, which he had grown along the trail the woman was walking. The Sun placed them directly in front of her and all around her, and the woman passed by them without paying any attention. She looked right at them and still did not see them. They squished between her toes as she walked, still she did not feel them.

So, the Sun made a large clump of blackberry bushes grow and put those directly on the trail the woman walked. They grew and grew, filled with blackberries.

The woman walked on, straight through the bushes, looking right at them but not seeing them, being brushed by them but not feeling them.

Next, the Sun created the most beautiful serviceberry trees, also called sugar plums, which stood beside the trail the woman walked, their branches creating a tunnel overhead with the beautiful, plump berries hanging low for her to reach. Still, the woman walked on. Even as she passed by and their scent filled the air, she could not smell them.

The Sun made all manner of other fruits and berries and set them and had them grow in, on, and around the trail the woman walked. But the woman did not look at them.

Finally, the Sun created a patch of the most succulent and beautiful, ripe strawberries. They were the first strawberries. When the woman came upon the strawberries, she stopped, and she gathered a few in her hands. As she picked and plucked the strawberries, she turned toward the west.

When she turned, the woman remembered the man. She turned back toward the Sunland, but she could not go on now that she had remembered the man. She could not go any farther.

The woman picked a few more of the strawberries and started walking again back on the trail. Away from the Sunland. As she walked, her husband came into view, still walking the trail, and they went back together." *

Salamander scurries up a log that has become stuck upon the riverbank. He looks at the coming bend in the river, where pink and white flower petals are drifting and swirling atop the surface.

"We have arrived at Samanalakanda, Dragonfly," says Salamander.

"That was not so long of a journey," says Dragonfly.

"It never does seem to take as long as one would think to arrive here," says Salamander.

"Is Butterfly here?" asks Dragonfly.

"All butterflies come here," says Salamander. "Go and see."

"Aren't you coming?" asks Dragonfly.

"Not today," says Salamander.

"I thought you wanted to eat me?" Dragonfly asks cautiously, with a slight chuckle in his voice.

"I'll come back when you're truly happy and see if my appetite has returned," says Salamander, looking Dragonfly in the eyes. "For now, I am satisfied."

Before Dragonfly can retort, Salamander dives into the river and disappears into its depths beneath the surface.

Dragonfly takes a deep breath, and then another and another, steadying himself for what he might find or not find. He flies slowly across the river to the bend, rounding it as it opens into a most beautiful sight.

As the river turns, it opens into a lagoon where three waterfalls empty into it, surrounded by lush greens and old cherry blossom trees all around crystalline waters. There are blossom petals, pink and white, the mists of the waterfalls creating hues of pinks, with lilies growing along the shore and lotus flowers of red, pink, blue, purple, and white growing atop the surface of the water.

Mixed in with the petals of the flowers, in the branches of the trees, drifting and fluttering and falling through the air are hundreds, perhaps thousands, of butterflies, singing sweet, soft sounds of nectar.

There, resting upon a purple lotus flower with a golden center, is one very particular Butterfly, still but breathing with a tear and a scorch mark upon her left wing.

Dragonfly gently hovers down to the flower and lands softly; he says not a word but looks upon her and caresses her wings and face as gently as he is able.

Butterfly slowly opens her eyes, looks up from her dreamy state, and smiles.

"You are Dragonfly," she whispers.

CHAPTER VIII

The Name of the Flower and the Tears of the River

Dragonfly looks Butterfly over, wincing as he sees her burnt wing, the tear cutting through her colorful patterns.

"Isn't it beautiful here?" asks Butterfly, her soft voice rising to meet Dragonfly, rousing him from his thoughts and feelings of guilt.

A fog filters over his eyes that he must shake away, and without taking his eyes from her, he looks at her face and her own eyes going from the trees to the other butterflies fluttering through the grotto, and he cannot help but smile at her wonderment.

"Never have I seen a more beautiful vision," he says, speaking barely above a whisper.

Butterfly shifts her weight just slightly to turn toward the waterfalls with their pink mists, and as she does, she gives out a sharp sigh of pain as she moves her wounded wing. Dragonfly feels as though he has been struck by the very lightning bolt that had sent the tree to cinder at hearing that sound. The guilt he feels becomes almost too much to bear. He closes his eyes as the fog of building water begins to creep over them. He takes a breath as he tries to say the words he wants to say; but they keep getting stuck in his throat.

"Butterfly," he finally manages to say; "this is all my—"

"Did I ever tell you about my eldest son?" asks Butterfly, seeming not to hear that Dragonfly is speaking to her.

"No," he says, held in near complete shock but steeling himself with a swallow and forcing himself to continue; "you didn't."

Butterfly lets out a long sigh, so long that Dragonfly holds his breath as his heart pounds.

"You remind me so much of him, Dragonfly," she says.

Dragonfly feels the water rising over his eyes and dares not blink as he pauses, says nothing, and lets a moment pass.

"I like it here," says Butterfly.

"Butterfly," says Dragonfly, swallowing again, the watery film over his eyes clouding his vision completely. "I'm so—"

"I think I'll stay," says Butterfly, interrupting him again.

Dragonfly swallows hard again and this time blinks away the watery film and fog, surprised and shocked at her words; but realizing he had already known. The water once again begins to well over his sight, and every time he blinks it away, it wells up again.

"You can't stay here, Butterfly," he says, unable to stop himself, "There are bats at night."

He says the words, attempting to make a joke and give her a laugh, but the words come out, instead, sounding as a plea.

"I'll hide and not go out at night, then," says Butterfly, giggling. "They will never see me."

Dragonfly cannot stop the swelling of water over his eyes as he smiles at her brave and cheeky response.

"But then you can't dance with the fireflies anymore," he says, continuing just to keep her talking so he may hear her soft and singsong voice a little longer. "And you're still on the river."

Again, Dragonfly notices his words ending with the sounds of pleading and near-desperation and longing. Butterfly giggles again, causing the swelling of water over Dragonfly's eyes to increase even more with the sound.

"I like the river," says Butterfly, her voice softer and quieter with each passing word. "It has everything I want."

"But the river isn't where we are going," says Dragonfly gently, but unable to shake that pleading tone from them.

Butterfly giggles again. This time, the sound comes out as a soft breathing whisper and her eyes begin to close.

"I forget where we were going," she says.

The watery film over Dragonfly's eyes now begins to roll down his face as the very air seems to tremble. Butterfly's choice of the word *were* instead of *are* does not go unnoticed by him.

"I didn't," he says, the words feeling as though they are choking the life out of him just to say them. "The river is only how we get there."

"Where were we going again?" she asks through a light smile, an inaudible giggle escaping her as she speaks so quietly Dragonfly can barely hear her as he leans as close to her face and lips as he can.

A gentle breeze begins to pick up around them, blowing the branches of the trees and sending the pink mist of the waterfalls spraying out around them in spiraling patterns, the leaves, petals, and flowers spinning and twirling through the air and upon the water's surface. The water fills Dragonfly's eyes increasingly as he looks down at her, and a single drop falls from his face and into the water below with a gentle *plop* of a sound.

"To the sea," says Dragonfly through choked words and heavy tears.

The breeze continues to blow, picking up speed, the swaying branches, leaves, and flowers of the cherry blossom making music, the rustle of butterfly wings fluttering through the air, the continuous sound of water cascading over rock and down the falls into the grotto's lagoon creating a chorus.

"Oh, yes," says Butterfly, whispering softly. "Now I remember. To find the Wind."

Dragonfly smiles. It was all he could do to keep from collapsing or flying away—anything to keep from feeling everything he was feeling in this moment. But he stays, and he looks upon Butterfly as the breeze picks up even more, and Butterfly's wings begin to flutter as flowers and blossom petals dance in the air around them.

"You can tell me the name of the flower now," says Butterfly.

Another rush of welling water fills his eyes and drop after drop falls from his face into the waters below. Dragonfly blinks and looks up and then back at Butterfly. He smiles at her as he takes a breath and matches his internal rhythm to hers, their heartbeats as one, slow and steady, and he takes one more deep breath from the core of the earth.

"They are named, Rose," he says as tenderly as he is able.

As he says the word, Butterfly lets out a sweet-sounding sigh, and once she finishes and goes silent, the two heartbeats that had felt as one, were now but one heartbeat, one rhythm. Not two.

The breeze becomes a gust of strong wind, and before Dragonfly can act, react, or respond, Butterfly is lifted into the air by the strong gust. Her delicate body is swirling through the air, being carried aloft by the current of wind. The other butterflies swirl and dance with her. Up, and up she flies, and down, and all around the grotto, over the mists of the waterfall, between the boulders, up, and up, and over, into the trees and forest. Dragonfly watches, barely able to see through the continuous pouring of tears from his eyes down his face and into the river below.

He watches the wind carry her and then suddenly, just as it seems she would be carried above the trees, into the sky and clouds, and what may lay beyond, she is stopped, seemingly in midair between two branches of a tree in the center of the three waterfalls.

Dragonfly blinks through the tears and peers closer, and then for the first time, he notices what is there between the branches of that tree.

A white and shimmering, funnel-shaped nest of familiar-looking webbing.

Immediately Dragonfly rises into the air, meaning to rip Butterfly's delicate body from the web that holds it, but then he stops and settles back down to the flower.

The tears well in his eyes again, but also, he smiles as he remembers their conversations.

Dragonfly looks on at the funneled web, as long spindly legs come from the center of the funnel and gently wrap Butterfly's body in a silken shroud of the weaving, and then Dragonfly sees the many fluffy sacs of eggs laid within and around the funneled web.

Dragonfly stays there in the grotto for many moments, taking in the visions that were Butterfly's final sights. He studies and looks at every flower, leaf, and petal, determined to let this scene stay transfixed and burned into his mind and memory. So that it, and she, may never be forgotten.

Time passes, and Dragonfly rises into the air. And he continues down the river.

As he flies away from that spot, the tears return, swelling in his eyes, and without blinking them away, they fall, drip after drop into the waters of the river below, sending out tiny ripples in all directions as he makes his way to the sea, alone.

CHAPTER IX

Change of Season and Direction

D ragonfly has lost track of time as it passes him by, traveling along the river, unable to shake the amount of guilt he feels. Even through the understanding and acceptance, he has feelings and thoughts of, *what if he had done something different? What if he hadn't been so focused on the flames? What if he hadn't been so excited by the storm? What if he had not taken Butterfly with him on his quest to find the wind? What if he had not transformed himself into a Dragonfly and had stayed a nymph? What if he hadn't come up from the depths of his lake and risen to the surface when he saw her beautiful colors and the sun's rays of light shining upon them, glimmering through the darkness that he had been so comfortable in for so long? What if he had not wanted change so intensely?*

So many "what ifs" flitter through Dragonfly's mind. *What if* had always been his fiercest ally, his curiosity and imagination providing him the greatest of adventures and cleverest ideas. Now, *what if* appears as his most devastating adversary, threatening to consume and destroy him in any given moment. Entrapped in the feelings of his own self-betrayal, he does not notice the chill in the air that signals the end of the late summer and has moved the seasons well into the autumn. So cold is it that Dragonfly's wings are stiff with frost every morning and evening as he continues along the river, day after day passing him by.

Still, the *what if*'s consume him more and more, and again, so focused is he on these thoughts and dreads and the fears that are creeping in upon him that Dragonfly has not noticed how wide the river has become. He stays near the shore more out of a habitual traveling path than for any reason that the river is opening more and more to where it would take him many moments now to cross from one bank to the other and would be quite dangerous.

Another day has passed, and on this day of deep thought and contemplation, Dragonfly shudders with a great chill. The air has grown colder on this day than any before. Dragonfly looks up to the sky to see if the Sun has gone behind the clouds, that he might find a ray of sunshine to bask in. When he looks up, he sees, just in time, the sun dipping below the horizon and the moon already visible in the blue-gray, purplish sky. Upon further inspection, Dragonfly also realizes that he has arrived at his destination.

Dragonfly stops flying, and hovering in midair, he looks down and sees rolling waves beneath him, loping onto the shore nearby. He looks outward, those waves growing larger, and larger, and out into the seemingly never-ending expansiveness of the sea.

Dragonfly shivers and shudders again as the wind chills him to his core, and he blankets the sands and hovers among the dunes and the tall grass here. Shielded by the dunes from the chill, Dragonfly nestles in among the grasses and looks out at the sea, at the waves, and tears fill his eyes as he thinks of Butterfly and what she would have been saying about the sea and the sight before him.

He tries to speak to her, but every time he thinks of her, all he can see is the burning tree. The flame upon her wing. Her eyes when she was falling into the rushing waters of the river, and her final wisp of breath as she passed beside the lotus. And her delicate body being carried by the wind, into the funneled web of the grotto spider and its offspring.

As he thinks all these things, he grows angry. He forgets his understanding of all the things and his learned knowledge, and he feels rage swelling within him.

Rage toward the Wind itself. Suddenly, the Wind is to blame for all.

It is much easier to be angry at the Wind and blame the Wind for all this heartache, this loss, and all the *what ifs*. So much easier, Dragonfly thinks as he lets his anger and rage grow and grow.

He wonders, why worry and be angry with himself over things he cannot control, when he can blame and be angry at the Wind? Full of fury, he decides he does not wish to simply question the Wind. Now, he demands answers, and he will not stop until he has them.

Dragonfly nearly becomes lost in his own anger and rage, his wings are buzzing furiously now, and the chill in the air is no longer a biting cold. He is filled with a rising heat and inner flame.

He is ready, he decides. He will fly out into the Sea, find the Wind, and demand the Wind answer for all it has caused.

He takes flight, determined to go off into and across the sea.

"Dragonfly, no," says an unknown but familiar voice.

The voice grabs ahold of him as if a hand has been placed upon him, and suddenly he is stunned and still, his wings unmoving and folded against him once again, the rage subsides for the moment and is replaced with curiosity and bewilderment.

Dragonfly looks around him, sure he had truly felt a hand or presence upon him.

"Look here, Dragonfly," speaks the voice.

Dragonfly feels the direction of the voice coming from above him. He looks out over the sea and up, and there is the Moon. Full and glorious and illuminated with an indigo-blue ring of immense light emanating from it so intensely that the night is nearly as bright as day.

"Traveler," says Dragonfly in a reverent whisper.

The auric glow of the Moon seems to shimmer brighter as he looks upon its surface in the night sky.

"I've been waiting for you to get here for quite some time, Dragonfly," says the Moon. "It took a lot longer to get you out of your lake than I had wished."

Dragonfly raises his eye and lowers the other, and the Moon lets out a laugh as he does.

"Tell me, Dragonfly, why are you so angry?" asks the Moon.

Dragonfly continues to look up into the glowing Moon. He wants to shout out all his rage and angers toward the Wind and what he has lost.

"I don't know," he says, the only words he can manage in this moment.

"That is an incredibly good place to start, Dragonfly," says the Moon, its glow brightening. "Why have you come all the way to the Sea?"

"To find the Wind," says Dragonfly.

"What do you want from the Wind?" asks the Moon.

"Answers," says Dragonfly.

"Ah," says the Moon. "I see."

"Where is the Wind?" asks Dragonfly, looking about him and returning his gaze upward, toward the Moon. "Grandfather said it would be here. Must I go into the sea?"

"The winds are here," says the Moon, the glow brightening and the surrounding stars shimmering in the sky; "but the Wind is elsewhere. Dear Dragonfly, no, you must not go into the sea now."

"To where, then?" asks Dragonfly, without a thought's hesitation.

"That is a question you must ask the Sun," says the Moon.

Dragonfly hangs his head in disappointment for a passing moment and returns his gaze upward.

"Do you know why the Wind would tell me one thing and tell Butterfly another?" he asks.

"Only the Wind knows why the Wind does what it does," says the Moon, allowing a moment of silence to pass, again, as Dragonfly reflects on the words.

"Don't fret, Dragonfly," continues the Moon. "The Sun will return soon and give you a new direction to follow to find the Wind and the answers you seek."

"Why did Butterfly have to die?" asks Dragonfly, keeping his gaze skyward with a sadness but curiosity within his voice.

"Life is not separate from death. It only looks that way,"* says the Moon, speaking with an echo, as if from an even farther distance than perceived, while at the same time, so close that it could have been a whisper in Dragonfly's ear, and even his own voice, within his mind.

Dragonfly settles upon the grass; the night chill has returned as his anger has fallen away. He huddles down lower between the tall grasses and the sandy dunes and looks upward into the night sky. It is full of stars and the bright and shining glow of the full moon.

"Here, Dragonfly, rest," says the Moon. "You have had a long journey to arrive at the beginning, and I have a story for you while you await the Sun's return."

Dragonfly takes a breath and holds himself still against the chilling air.

"Among the tribes of the two-legged people, their chief god is the Sun," says the Moon with a voice of echoing melody. "In their eyes, the Sun made the world and rules over it, and it is to the Sun that they pray.

The Sun has many names to the two-legged people and one of them is 'Old Man.' Beware, though, there is another 'Old Man' who is vastly different from the Sun, and instead of being great, wise, and wonderful, that Old Man is foolish, mean, and contemptible.

Every summer, when the berries ripen, the two-legged tribes would hold a great festival with sacrifice and named it the Ceremony of the Medicine Lodge.

It was a festival of happy meetings, many feasts, and giving of gifts. When those who wished to have good luck in their undertakings would prove their prayers to the Old Man, the Sun, were sincere by sacrificing their bodies and torturing themselves in ways of great suffering.

In the ancient times, these happenings occurred among many of the two-legged tribes all over the entire world.

Soon after these times, those called the Raven Bearers held a dance. They painted themselves and wore their finest ornaments while each one tried to out dance the other.

During the dance, the men would ask the chief for his daughter's hand, and to each one she would say, 'No.'

After the Raven Bearers, came the Bulls to dance. And then the Kit-Foxes. And all the tribes of the One Nation held their dances. The rich men and the great warriors would ask the chief for his daughter's hand, but to everyone, she would say, 'No.'

After so many, her father, the chief, became angry.

'Why is this?' asked the chief of his daughter. 'All of the best men have asked for you, and still, you say 'No."

'Father, listen to me,' said the girl to her father. 'The above person, the Sun, said to me: *Do not marry any of these men, for you belong to me. Listen to what I say, and you shall be happy and live to a great age.* Again, he spoke to me and said: *Take heed, you must not marry; you are mine.'*

'Ah!' shouted her father. 'It must always be as the Sun says.' And so, they spoke no more about the men asking for her hand.

Among the tribe there was a poor young man. He was extremely poor. His father, mother, and all his relations were gone. He had no lodge and no wife to tan his robes or make his moccasins. His clothes were always old and worn. He had no home. One day he would sleep in one lodge, then the next, he ate and slept in another. Thus, he lived. The young man had a good face, but on his cheek was a bad scar.

One summer, after the tribes had their dances, some of the other young men met this poor Scarface, and they laughed at him.

'Why do you not ask the chief's daughter to marry you?' they called to him. 'You are so rich and handsome!'

The others mocked and laughed. Scarface did not laugh but only looked at them.

'I will do as you say,' said Scarface. 'I shall go and ask her.'

All the others and the young men thought this was funny; they laughed a great deal at Scarface as he walked away toward the river. He waited there, near the place where the women would come to get water.

He would wait and watch the other women gather water, until finally, the chief's daughter came there.

'Girl, stop, please,' said Scarface to the girl. 'I want to speak with you. I do not wish to do anything secretly, but I speak to you here, openly, where the Sun looks down and all may see.'

The girl looked at Scarface.

'Speak, then,' said the girl.

'I have seen the days,' said Scarface. 'I have seen how you have refused all those men, who are young, rich, and brave. Today, some of those young men laughed at me and said to me: *Why do you not ask her?* I am poor. I have no lodge, no food, no clothes, no robes. I have no relations. All of them are gone. Yet now, today, I say to you. Be my wife.'

The girl hid her face in her robe and brushed the ground with the point of her moccasin, back and forth, back, and forth, for she was thinking.

'It is true,' she said. 'I have refused all those rich, young men, yet now a poor one asks me, and I am glad. You are poor, but that does not matter. My father will give you dogs. My mother will make us a lodge. My relations will give us robes and furs. You will no longer be poor.'

Then the young man was glad, and he started forward to kiss her, but she put out her hand and held him back.

'Wait,' she said; 'the Sun has spoken to me. He said I may not marry, that I belong to him. That if I listen to him, I shall live to great age. So, I say, go to the Sun. Say to him: *She whom you spoke with has listened to your words. She has never done wrong, but now, she wants to marry. I want her for my wife.*

Ask him to take that scar from your face. That will be his sign, and I shall know he is pleased. But, if he refuses, or if you cannot find his lodge, then do not return to me.'

'Oh!' cried Scarface. 'At first your words were good. I was glad. Now it is dark, and my heart is dead. Where is the Sun's far-off lodge? Where even is the trail that no one has yet traveled or found?'

'Take courage, take courage,' said the girl softly, and off she went to her lodge.

Scarface was now unhappy and did not know what to do. He sat down and covered his face with his robes and tried to think.

Finally, he stood up and went to an old woman who had been kind to him.

'Forgive me for what I ask,' he said to her. 'I am extremely poor, and I am going on a long journey. Will you please make me some moccasins?'

'Where are you going?' asked the woman. 'Is it far from camp?'

'I do not know where I am going,' said Scarface. 'I am in trouble; but I cannot talk about it.'

The old woman had a kind heart, so she made him several pairs of moccasins and gave him a pack of food containing pemmican, dried meats, and back fat.

All alone, and with a sad heart, Scarface climbed the bluff that overlooked the valley of the tribes, and when he reached the top, he peered over the cliff face and looked down at the camp. He wondered if he would ever see it again, if he would return to the girl and the people.

'O Sun, forgive me my requests and demands,' he prayed, and turning away from the camp and the people, he set off to seek the trail to the Sun's lodge.

For many days he went on, crossing great prairies and followed up timbered rivers and crossed the steep mountains. As each day passed, his pack grew lighter and lighter. He looked for berries and roots and sometimes would kill an animal, and these things gave him food.

One chilly night, he came to the den of a great wolf.

'*Huhahh*!' said the Wolf. 'What are you doing here, so far from your home?'

'I am seeking the lodge of the Sun,' said Scarface. 'I have been sent to speak with him.'

The Wolf looked Scarface up and down.

'I have traveled over much of the nation,' said the Wolf. 'I know all the prairies, the valleys, and the mountains; but I have never seen the Sun's Lodge. But wait a moment. I know one of the people who is incredibly wise, and who may be able to show you the path to the Sun's lodge. Go, and ask the Bear.'

After sharing a night of rest and a meal with the great Wolf, Scarface went on again, stopping here and there to pick berries. When night fell, he came upon the Bear's lodge.

'Where is your home?' asked the Bear. 'Why are you traveling so far alone?'

'Ah. I have come to you for help,' said Scarface. 'Forgive me, because of the girl and what she has asked of me, I am looking for the Sun. I wish to ask him for her hand.'

The Bear looked at Scarface from head to toe.

'I do not know where the Sun's lodge is,' said the Bear. 'I have traveled by the many rivers, and I know the highest mountains, yet I have never seen his lodge. Farther up the path is one of the people. The stripe-faced one. He knows a great deal; go and ask him.'

Scarface shared a night of rest and a meal with the great Bear and continued the next day. By midday he came upon a hole and there was the Badger.

'Oh, cunning striped face!' Scarface called out. 'I wish to speak with you.'

The Badger brought his head out of his hole and looked at Scarface.

'What do you want, my brother?' said the Badger.

'I wish to find the Sun's lodge,' said Scarface. 'I wish to speak with him.'

The Badger looked up at Scarface from his hole.

'I do not know where he lives,' said the Badger. 'I never travel extremely far. Over there in the forest is the Wolverine. He is always traveling about and knows many things. Perhaps he can tell you.'

Scarface thanked the Badger, turned, and went into the forest and looked all about for the Wolverine. He searched and sought over and under and all throughout the forest and woods but could not see him. He looked and looked but could not find the Wolverine. Finally, exhausted, Scarface sat down on a log to rest and spoke out loud.

'Alas, Wolverine! Forgive me and take pity. My food is gone, my moccasins are worn out, and I fear I shall die.'

'What is it, my brother?' asked a voice remarkable close to him.

Scarface looked around and saw the Wolverine sitting at the end of the log beside him.

'She whom I wish to marry belongs to the Sun,' said Scarface. 'I am trying to find his lodge so that I may ask him for her.'

The Wolverine looked at Scarface.

'Ah, I know where the Sun's lodge is,' said the Wolverine. 'It is becoming night now, but tomorrow I will show you the trail and the path to the big water. The Sun lives on the other side of it.'

After a night of rest and a meal, early in the morning, the two set out together. The Wolverine showed Scarface the trail. Scarface bowed and thanked him and then he followed the path until he came to the water's edge.

When he looked out over it, his heart nearly stopped. Never had anyone seen such a great water. The other side could not be seen, and there was no ending to it.

Scarface sat down on the shore and thought to himself that this was the end. His food was all gone; his moccasins were worn out and no more; he had no strength left, no courage to be found; his heart was sick and sad; and he spoke to himself.

I cannot return to the people. Here, by this water, I shall die.

Just as he was thinking these thoughts, two swans came swimming up to the shore.

'Why have you come here?' said one swan.

'What are you doing?' said the other swan.

'It is extremely far to the place where your people live,' said the swans together.

Scarface looked at the swans.

'I have come here to die,' he said. 'Far away in my country is a beautiful girl. I want to marry her, but she belongs to the Sun. So, I have set out to find him and ask him for her. I have traveled many days. My food is gone. I cannot go back. I cannot cross this great water. So here, I must die.'

The swans looked to each other and then to Scarface.

'No,' said the first swan.

'It shall not be so,' said the other.

'Across this great water is the lodge of the Above Person,' said the two swans together. 'Get on our backs, and we will take you there.'

Scarface stood up immediately. He felt strong and full of courage again. He waded out into the water and lay down on the swans' backs, and they swam away.

It was a fearful journey, full of terrors, for that great water was deep and black, and in it lived strange peoples and great animals that could and might reach up at any moment and seize a person, pulling them down under the water.

Yet the swans carried Scarface safely to the other side. There was seen a broad, hard trail and winding path leading back from the water's edge and shore.

'There,' spoke the swans. 'You are now close to the Sun's Lodge. Follow that trail and path, and soon, you will see it.'

Scarface bowed and thanked the swans, and he began to walk the trail as they flew back across the great water. After he had gone a little way, he came upon some beautiful things lying on the trail.

There was a war shirt, a shield, a bow, and a quiver of arrows. Scarface had never seen such fine weapons. He looked at them and admired them for their beauty and exquisiteness, but he did not touch them, and at last, he walked around them and moved on.

A little farther up the path, he saw a young man. An extremely handsome person. His hair was long, his clothing was made of strange skins, and his moccasins were sewed with bright feathers he had never seen.

'Did you see some weapons lying in the trail back there?' asked the strange young man as Scarface approached.

'Yes,' replied Scarface, 'I saw them.'

The young man looked behind Scarface, down the path, and then into his eyes.

'Did you touch them?' asked the young man.

'No,' said Scarface. 'I supposed someone had left them there, and I did not touch them.'

'Ah,' said the young man, clapping his hands together. 'You do not meddle with the property of others. What is your name, and where are you going?'

Scarface told him who he was and where he was going and why.

'My name is Early Riser, *the Morning Star*,' said the young man. 'The Sun is my father. Come, I will take you to our lodge. My father is not at home now, but he will return at night as he always does.'

After a long walk through the trail and path, at length, they came to the lodge. It was large and handsome and beautiful, and on it were painted many strange medicine animals. Some Scarface knew and some he did not.

On a tripod behind the lodge were the Sun's weapons and his war clothing. Scarface felt ashamed and unworthy to go into the lodge, and Morning Star recognized this.

'Friend, do not be afraid,' said Morning Star. 'We are glad you have come.'

When they entered the lodge, a woman was sitting inside. She was the Moon, the Sun's wife, and the mother of Morning Star.

She gave him food to eat and waited for him to finish his meal.

'Why have you come so far from your people?' asked the Moon, speaking kindly to Scarface.

Scarface then told her of the beautiful girl that he wished to marry.

'She belongs to the Sun,' he said. 'I have come to ask him for her.'

When it was nearly night and time for the Sun to return, the Moon hid Scarface under a pile of robes in the back of the lodge.

'A strange person is here,' said the Sun as soon as he arrived at the doorway.

'Yes, Father,' said Morning Star. 'A young man has come to see you. He is a good man, for he found some of my things in the trail, on the path, and did not touch them.'

Scarface, then, came out from under the robes, and the Sun entered the lodge and sat down, and he looked at Scarface.

'I am glad you have come to our lodge,' said the Sun. 'Stay with us for as long as you like. Sometimes my son is lonely. Be his friend.'

The next day, the two young men were talking about going hunting.

'Go with my son wherever you like,' said the Moon to Scarface; 'but do not hunt near the big water. Do not let him go there. That is the home of the Great Birds with long, sharp beaks. They kill people. I have had many sons, but these great birds have killed them all. Only Morning Star is left.'

Scarface stayed an exceptionally long time in the Sun's lodge, and every day he went hunting with Morning Star. One day, they went near the big water, and they saw the Great Birds.

Morning Star spoke out to Scarface in a hushed and excited whisper.

'Come on,' he said. 'Let us go and kill those Great Birds.'

'No, no,' whispered Scarface. 'We must not go there. Those birds are terrible, and they will kill us.'

Morning Star did not and would not listen. He ran toward the big water, and so Scarface after him, for he knew he must kill the Great Birds and save the boy's life.

He ran ahead of Morning Star as fast as he could and met the terrible Great Birds, which were ready and coming to fight. Scarface killed every one of them with his spear. Not even one was left.

The two young men cut off the heads of the Great Birds and carried them home, and when Morning Star's mother heard what they had done and they then showed her the Great Bird's heads, she was glad. She wept and cried and whooped over the two young men and called Scarface, 'My son.'

When the Sun came home at night, she told him about it, and he, too, was glad, and he looked at Scarface.

'My son, I will not forget what you have this day done for me,' said the Sun. 'Tell me now, what I can do for you. What is your trouble?'

'Alas,' said Scarface. 'Forgive me; take pity. I came here to ask you for that beautiful girl. I want to marry her. I asked her and she was glad, but she says that she belongs to you and that you told her not to marry.'

'What you say is true,' said the Sun to Scarface. 'I have seen the days and all that she has done. Now, I give her to you. She is yours. I am glad that she has been wise, and I know that she has never done wrong.'

The Sun takes care of good women; they shall live a long time, and so shall their husbands and children.

'Now, soon you will go home,' continued the Sun. 'I wish to tell you something, and you must be wise and listen. I am the only chief; everything is mine; I made the earth, the mountains, the prairies, the rivers, and the forests. I made the people and all the animals. This is why I say that I alone am chief. I can never die. It is true that the winter makes me old and weak, but every summer I grow young again.

What one of the animals is the smartest?' the Sun asked and then went on, 'It is the Raven. For he always finds food and he is never hungry.

Which of the animals is the most to be reverenced?' asked the Sun and then went on, 'It is the Buffalo. Of all the animals, I like him best. He is for the people; he is your food and your shelter.

What part of his body is sacred?' asked the Sun and then went on, 'It is the tongue. That belongs to me.

What else is sacred?' asked the Sun and then went on, 'Berries. They, too, are mine. Come with me now and see the world.'

The Sun then took Scarface to the edge of the sky, and they looked down and saw the world.

'It is flat, and round, and all around the edge it goes straight down. Then, if any man is sick or in danger, his wife may promise to build me a lodge, so he recovers. If the woman is good, then I shall be pleased and help the man, but if she is not good, or if she lies, then I shall be angry.

You shall build the lodge like the world—round, with walls. But first, you must build a sweat lodge of one hundred sticks. It shall be arched like the sky, and one half of it shall be painted red, for me. The other half you shall paint black, for the night.'

The Sun told Scarface all about making the medicine lodge, and when he had finished speaking, he rubbed some medicine on the young man's face, and the scar that had been there disappeared.

The Sun gave the young man two Raven feathers.

'These are a sign for the girl that I give her to you,' said the Sun. 'They must always be worn by the husband of the woman who builds a medicine lodge.'

Now Scarface was ready to return home. The Sun and Morning Star gave him many good gifts; the Moon cried and kissed him and was sorry to see him go. Then the Sun showed him the short trail and path. It was the Wolf Road—*the Milky Way*. He followed the path and trail, and soon he reached the ground.

The day was extremely hot when Scarface arrived back near the camp of the tribes. All the lodge skins were raised, and the people were sitting in the shade. There was a chief, a generous man, who all day long was calling out for feasts, and people kept coming to his lodge to eat and smoke tobacco with him. Early in the morning, this chief was sitting nearby a person close-wrapped in their robe. All day long this person sat there and did not move.

When it was nearly night, the chief turned to the other.

'That person has sat there all day in the strong heat, wrapped in his robe, and he has not eaten nor drunk,' said the chief. 'Perhaps he is a stranger. Go and ask him to come to my lodge.'

Some of the young men of the tribe ran up to the stranger.

'Why have you sat here all day in the great heat all alone?' they asked. 'Come to the shade of the lodges. The chief asks you to eat and smoke tobacco with him.'

The stranger rose and threw off his robe, and the young men were surprised. The stranger wore fine clothing; his bow, shield, and other weapons were of strange make, but then they realized they knew his face. They saw him as Scarface, although his scar was gone.

So, the young men ran ahead to the camp.

'The scar-faced poor young man has returned,' they shouted. 'He is poor no longer. The scar on his face is gone.'

All the people of the tribes hurried out to see him and to ask him questions.

'Where did you get all these fine things?' they asked.

Scarface did not answer. There, in the crowd, stood the beautiful young woman. Scarface walked over to her, and taking the two Raven feathers from his head, he gave them to her.

'The trail was long, and I nearly died,' said Scarface; 'but by those helpers I found the Sun's lodge. He is glad. He sends these feathers to you. They are the sign.'

Great was her gladness then. They were married and made the first medicine lodge together, as the Sun had said.

The Sun was glad. He gave them great age. They were never sick. When they were extremely old, one morning their children called out to them, 'Awake, rise, and eat.'

They did not move.

In the night, together, in sleep and without pain, their shadows had departed to the *Sandhills*." *

Dragonfly looks across the sea as the Moon is descending now beneath the horizon. The Moon's reflection mirrored upon the surface, tears well over his eyes, and begin to fall down his face into the sands of the dunes below.

"Dragonfly, why do you cry?" asks the Moon, softly.

"Is the Sun, the Wind, the Sea, the Storm, the Earth," says Dragonfly, quietly with a slight trembling in his voice; "are you angry with me?"

The brightness of the Moon pulses and shimmers as it appears to sink beneath the waves of the sea.

"Why would any be angry with you?" asks the Moon in a whisper of a voice.

The tears fall more and more, nearly uncontrollably, down Dragonfly's face to the sands below.

"Because I killed Butterfly," he says quietly, with a heaviness that weighs more than anything he has felt before in his lifetime.

The glow of the Moon pulses and shimmers again across the surface of the Sea, as the last of its light may be seen.

"Please, don't leave me," says Dragonfly in a delicate whisper.

"I am never far, Dragonfly," says the voice of the Moon as it disappears beneath the waves and beyond the horizon, the words echoing all around and through him. "I am here. Rest now and wait for the Sun's return; it is near."

The final glow descends beneath the waves into the depth of the Sea. The sky darkens, and the chill in the air increases, sending shivers throughout Dragonfly's body as he clutches tighter to the reeds that he rests upon within the dunes of the seashore. He sits there for moments uncounted, contemplating and remembering his memories, thinking his thoughts.

Warmth cuts through the chill. It begins low and rises and across his back until the warmth falls over his head, bringing calm and stillness to the shivering he felt within the cold night's air.

Dragonfly lifts his head and looks behind him, and he sees the early morning rising of the Sun, cresting as a wondrous event, occurring just now, over the horizon.

CHAPTER X

An Ending and a Beginning

"Good morning, Sun," says Dragonfly, over the sounds of the crashing waves rushing onto the shore and pulling back out to the sea, and over the sound of the breeze blowing through the grasses of the dunes.

"Good morning, Dragonfly," says the Sun.

With a jolt but without surprise, Dragonfly both hears and feels the words near and around him, he peers into the soft glow emanating from the Sun, in the morning light when it is still possible to look upon it without harming the eyes.

"Great Sun, why is it that even now I can feel the Wind all around me?" asks Dragonfly. "I can sense and even see it when it picks up grains of sand from the dunes and swirls them around through the air. I can feel it in the tickling of the tall grasses as they sway back and forth against my wings, scales, and limbs. I can see it in the swelling surface of the waters, the breaks, and waves of the Sea. Why is it that the Wind is all around, and it is here, but it will not speak to me as it once did? Is the Wind angry with me?"

Dragonfly does not take his eyes away from the rising Sun as he awaits the response.

"No, Dragonfly," says the Sun. "The Wind is not angry with you. The wind you see and feel all around you is but the winds of the Wind—the gusts and breezes that the Wind sends to carry you to places it wishes you to seek and find. I suggest you keep sensing them and see where they take you."

"Where are they to take me now?" asks Dragonfly. "I had thought the Sea was the destination where I would find the Wind."

"Dear Dragonfly, you are not yet ready to cross into or over the great Sea," says the Sun. "You would not survive the trip in the state you are now in. Don't fret; the time will come."

"When?" asks Dragonfly. "How will I know when I am ready?"

"You will remember," says the Sun.

"How?" asks Dragonfly.

"There is somewhere, first, you must go before your wings will be strong enough to carry you across the great Sea," echoes the Sun as it rises higher into the sky.

"Where must I go?" Dragonfly asks curiously.

"We are nearing the end of autumn," says the Sun. "There is but a short distance west you must travel when you leave here and then to the north for the winter."

"To the north for the winter?" asks Dragonfly, confused, and nearly panicked. "Is it not colder in the north? Won't I freeze?"

"Travel north, Dragonfly, until you come upon the great Desert Valley," says the Sun. "There you will spend your winter. There will be cold and dark nights filled with all manner of soul and spirit, but nay, you will not freeze."

The Sun beams its radiating light, and warmth falls over Dragonfly, removing the last of the chill from the night and early morning.

"Will you be there?" asks Dragonfly, looking into the sun's still muted light.

"Is there anywhere you have been that I have not?" asks the Sun with a gentle laugh.

Dragonfly pauses for a moment, thinking.

"The night," he says.

"Clever," says the Sun with another laugh. "Though, even in the night, I am there. You simply cannot see me from where you are."

Dragonfly contemplates on this for another moment.

"How can you, the Sun, be somewhere and not be seen?" he asks.

"If I could be seen in the night," says the Sun; "then it wouldn't be called the night, would it? And then you would never see the Moon. The Moon is a most beautiful sight to behold, is it not?"

"I adore the Moon most of all," says Dragonfly, nodding in agreement and bowing his head. "My apologies, great Sun."

"Don't apologize," says the Sun, with a gentle chuckle and a great sigh. "It is a shared sentiment between you and me. The Moon is more special to me than any could ever know. There is but only one like the Moon and as much as I love, adore, and desire the Moon, I may never touch her, always out of my reach, coming as I go, departing as I arrive.

A circle-walk and a dance shared between her and me. She is as a snowflake to my flame, unique and special and one of a kind, but if even for a moment we touch or kiss, her intricate form and design will melt into a puddle and then poof into a vapor of steam, rising into the cosmos unseen.

Until the day comes when we both are ready to join the unseen, we continue our dance, grateful for the moments we get to look upon one another from afar in those moments in between when the world is sleeping and awake."

Dragonfly pauses without saying a word, listening intently, as if he was just gifted with one of the greatest secrets ever told. He says not a word and asks not a single question but listens and feels moved.

The Sun beams again, its light getting brighter as it rises higher into the morning sky.

"When we pass the midday afternoon," continues the Sun; "you may follow me for a way to the west. When I have set this day behind us and the Moon rises again, turn to the north and find the Desert Valley. It will be a difficult journey, Dragonfly, even more difficult than what you have seen and faced to come here, to this place, here and now."

Dragonfly gulps at the thought, his courage wavering for a moment, his wings flutter, his body shivers, and he inhales, holds, and exhales. He remains determined and decided. He will go through this Desert Valley with its cold, dark nights filled with souls and spirits. He will see what is to be seen and learn what is to be learned.

"Here, now, we will pass the time to midday with a story," says the Sun. "You have heard the tale of 'How the World Was Made,' yes?"

Dragonfly nods, pauses, and looks at the Sun.

"Did you make the World?" he asks.

"The All made the World and all," says the Sun, beaming brighter. "I assisted and did my part as do all within the all. There are many stories from many tribes, nations, and peoples all over the world, here and others. Here I will tell you where the story of how the world was made, as you have heard it, comes from. Listen close, Dragonfly."

The Sun beams again, the sky is a myriad hue of blues and purples, oranges, reds, and yellows with translucently golden rays sprawled across the land.

"In the beginning, there was water everywhere," says the Sun. "Nothing else was to be seen. Then, there was something to be seen floating on the waves—a raft, and on this raft was Old Man and all the animals.

Old Man wished to make land, so he told the Beaver to dive down to the bottom of the water and to try to bring up a little mud.

The Beaver dived down, deep, and was under water for an extremely long time, but he could not reach the bottom.

Then, the Loon tried but could not reach the bottom.

After the Loon, the Otter tried, but the water was too deep.

At last, the Muskrat was sent down, and he was gone for the longest time, so long that they all thought he must be drowned and dead.

At last, the Muskrat floated to the top of the waves, extremely near to death, and when they pulled him up onto the raft and looked at his paws, there they found a small amount of mud held within them.

Old Man dried this mud, and he scattered it over the water, and so land was formed.

After the land had been made, Old Man traveled about on it, making things and fixing things up on the earth to suit and please him.

First, he marked out places where he wished the river to run, sometimes making them run smoothly and in some places, putting great falls and rapids on them.

He made the mountains and the prairie, the timber, forests, woods, and the small trees, bushes, and grasslands, and sometimes he carried along with him a lot of rocks, and from these he built some of the mountains and the Sweet Grass Hills.

These stand out from the prairie all by themselves.

Old Man caused the grasses to grow tall and high on the plains so that the animals might have something to feed on.

He marked off certain pieces of land where he caused different kinds of roots and all manner of berries to grow—a place for the camas root and lily; one for the carrots; one for the wild turnips, sweet roots, and bitter roots; one for serviceberries and sugarplums, bull berries, cherries, plums, and rosebuds.

Old Man made all kinds of animals that travel on the ground.

When he made the bighorn with its great horns, he placed them out on the prairie.

It did not seem to travel easily there; it was awkward and could not go fast, so he took it by one of its horns and led it up into the rough hills and among the rocks and let it go there, and it skipped about among the cliffs and easily went up fearful places.

'This is the place for you,' said Old Man to the bighorn; 'this is what you are fitted for—the rough country and the mountains.'

While he was in the mountains, Old Man made the antelope and turned it loose to see how it traveled.

The antelope ran so fast that it fell over some rocks and hurt itself. He saw that this would not do and took the antelope down on the prairie and set it free there, and it ran away fast and gracefully.

'This is the place that suits you,' Old Man said to the antelope.

At last, one day, Old Man decided that he would make a woman and a child, and he modeled some clay from the riverbank.

He made the shapes in human form and put them on the ground.

'You shall be people,' he said to the clay.

Old Man spread his robe over the clay figures and went away. The next morning, he went back to the place and lifted the robe and saw that the clay shapes had changed a little. When he looked again the next morning, they had changed even more.

And on the fourth day when he went to look at the clay figures, he lifted the robe.

'Stand up and walk,' he said to the clay.

And so, they did. They walked down to the river with he who had made them, he told them his name, and they stood there looking out at the water as it flowed by.

'How is it?' the woman asked Old Man. 'Shall we live always? Will there be no end to us?'

'I had not thought of this,' said the Old Man, looking at the woman. 'We must decide it. I will take this buffalo chip and throw it in the river. If it floats, people will become alive again four days after they have died; they will die for four days only. But if it sinks, there will be an end to people.'

Old Man threw the chip into the river, and it floated.

Old Man went to clap his hands when the woman turned and picked up a stone.

'No,' she said. 'I will throw this stone in the river. If it floats, we shall live always. If it sinks, people must die, so that their friends who are left alive may always remember them.'

The woman threw the stone in the water, and it sank.

'Well, you have chosen,' said Old Man. 'There will be an end to people.'

And Old Man clapped his hands together and walked away from the riverbank.

Not many nights after, the woman's child died, and the woman cried and cried a great deal.

'Let us change this,' she said to Old Man. 'The Law that you first made, let that be the Law.'

Old Man looked at the woman and wiped a tear from her cheek.

'Not so,' he said to her. 'What is made Law must be Law. We will undo nothing that we have done. The child is dead, but it cannot be changed. People will have to die.'

These first of the people did not have hands like a person; they had hands like a bear, with long claws. They were poor and naked and did not know how to make a living.

Old Man showed them the roots and the berries and showed them how to gather these and told them how, at certain times of the year, they should peel the bark off some of the trees and eat it, and that the little animals that live in the ground—the rats, squirrels, skunks, and beavers—were all good to eat.

He also taught them something about the roots that were good for medicines to cure sicknesses, ailments, and injuries of all kinds.

In those days there were buffalo, and these black animals were armed with long horns. Once, as the people were moving from here to there, the buffalo saw them and rushed upon them, hooked them with their long horns, killed them, and then ate them.

One day, Old Man was traveling about, and he came upon some of his children that he had made, lying there dead in the fields. They were torn to shreds and pieces and partially eaten by the buffalo. When he saw this, he felt guilty; he felt bad.

'I have not made these people right,' he said to himself. 'I will change this. From now on, the people shall eat the buffalo.'

Old Man went to some of the people that yet lived.

'How is it that you do nothing to these animals that are killing you?' he asked them.

'What can we do?' replied the people. 'The animals are armed and can kill us. We have no way to kill them.'

'That is not so hard,' said Old Man. 'I will make you something that will kill these animals.'

He went out right away and cut some straight shoots from the serviceberry trees, brought them in, and peeled the bark from them.

He took a larger piece of wood and flattened it, tied a string to it, and made a bow. Now, as he was the master of all birds, he went out and caught one, took the feathers from its wings, and tied them to the shaft of wood.

He tied four feathers along the shaft and tried the arrow at a mark and found that it did not fly well.

He took off the four feathers and put on three, and when he tried it at the mark again, he found that it went straight.

He then picked up some hard stones and broke sharp pieces from them. When he tried them, he found that the black flint stones made the best arrow points.

Old Man took these things to the people and showed them how to use them.

'The next time you go out,' Old Man said to the people; 'take these things with you and use them as I tell you. Do not run from these animals. When they rush at you and have come close, shoot the arrows at them as I have taught you, and you will see that they will run from you or will run around you in a circle.'

Old Man broke off pieces of stone, fixed them in a handle, and told the people that when they kill the buffalo that they should cut up the flesh with the stone knives.

When some of the people went on a little hill to look about, the buffalo saw them.

'Ah, there is some more of our food!' called the buffalo to each other, and then rushed upon the people.

The people did not run and began to shoot at the buffalo with the bows and arrows that had been given them, and the buffalo hit with an arrow felt it prick him.

'Oh, my friends,' cried the buffalo to his fellows; 'a great fly is biting me!'

With the flint knives that had been given to them, they cut up the bodies of the dead buffalo, and then Old Man came to them.

'It is not healthful to eat raw flesh,' he said. 'I will show you something better than that.'

He gathered soft, dry, rotten wood and made punk of it, took a piece of wood, and drilled a hole in it with an arrow point, and gave them a pointed piece of hardwood. He then showed them how to make a fire with fire sticks and how to cook the flesh of animals.

Afterward, the people found a certain sort of stone in the land and took another harder stone, working one upon the other and hollowing out the softer one, and made of it a kettle.

Old Man also made people and animals at another place and in another way. At the mountains, he made other earthen images of people and blew breath on the images, and they became people. They were men and women.

'What are we to eat?' they asked Old Man after a time.

Then he took more earth and made many images in the form of buffalo, and when he had blown on them, they stood up, and he made signs to them, and they started to run.

'There is your food,' he told the people.

'How are we to kill those animals?' asked the people.

'I will show you,' said Old Man.

He took them to the edge of a cliff and showed them how to heap up piles of stone, running back from the cliff, with the point of the V toward the cliff.

'Now, hide behind the piles of stones,' he told the people; 'and when I lead the buffalo this way, when they are opposite of you, stand up.'

Old Man went on toward the herd of buffalo and began to call them. The buffalo started toward him and followed him until they were inside the arms of the V. Then he ran to one side and hid, and as the people rose, the buffalo ran on in a straight line and jumped over the cliff, and some of them were killed by the fall.

'There, go and take the flesh of those animals.' Old Man said to the people.

Then, they tried to do so. They tried to tear the limbs off but could not. They tried to bite pieces out of the bodies but could not.

Old Man went to the edge of the cliff and broke some pieces of stone with sharp edges and showed them how to cut the flesh with these. From the buffalo that went over the cliff, some were not yet dead but only hurt, and they could not run away. The people cut strips of green hide and tied heavy stones in the middle, and with these called hammers, they broke in the skulls of the buffalo and killed them.

When they had taken the skins from these animals, they set up poles and put the hides over them and so made a shelter to sleep under.

In much later times, Old Man marked off a piece of land for the five tribes of the nation.

'When people come to cross this line at the border of your land," Old Man told the people; 'take your bows and arrows, your lances, and your war clubs, and give them battle, and keep them out. If they gain a footing here, trouble for you will follow.'" *

Dragonfly looks toward the sky where the light of the Sun has become much too bright to look directly into. The overlarge orange ball that is low in the sky is now directly overhead, smaller but yellow and intense as his eyes drift near it.

Dragonfly, instead, bows his head and lets the warmth wash over him.

"Great Sun, are you Old Man?" he asks.

"I have had so many names," says the Sun with a sigh; "and I will have so many more through the times. Just as the story will have many more beginnings and endings. All different, but all very much the same."

"I do enjoy all the stories," says Dragonfly with a whisper and a nod.

The Sun beams, and Dragonfly feels the warmth cascading over the back of his scales, and his wings flutter as he hovers above the reed, looking out to the sea, whose waters have become still, glassy, and shimmering with sparkles and gleams of light dancing upon the barely visible waves.

"As do I," confesses the Sun.

Dragonfly begins flying over the dunes, along the coast toward the Sun as it begins its descent to the western horizon. Dragonfly continues to look out over the sea as he flies along the coast, enjoying the sight of its stillness and immense vastness that seems never ending.

"Great Sun?" Dragonfly asks. "What is life?"

Though the Sun's rays are warm, there is still a noticeable chill in the air. The voiceless winds gust and swirl the sands of the dunes, and multicolored leaves from the nearby forest blow and dance up in the air, settling down and creating a blanket of reds, yellows, oranges, and browns amid the green, tall grasses and sands of the shore, with the green and blue of the sea lapping upward with the tide, just below Dragonfly's path of flight.

"It is the flash of a firefly in the night," says the Sun. "It is the breath of a buffalo in the wintertime. It is the little shadow that runs across the grass and loses itself in the sunset."*

Dragonfly continues flying toward the setting Sun, its brightness calming as it descends toward the western horizon. The once bright-blue sky now becoming a painted landscape of purples, blues, oranges, pinks, and reds.

Dragonfly looks up and notices they have come to a jetty along the shore. Large black rocks line the river in rows along each shore of the narrow channel, tumbling out into and beneath the Sea.

"These rocks here are obsidian, Dragonfly," says the Sun as it continues its descent toward the earth. "A mixture of fire and water made earthen. Follow them north to the Desert, and we will speak again. Be brave in the cold, dark nights amid the souls and spirits. Remember who you are, Dragonfly."

"Great Sun, what is Death?" asks Dragonfly, looking upon the solid, smooth, blackened rocks, preparing to begin his flight northward.

"Life is not separate from death," says the Sun in a voice that echoes through Dragonfly. "It only looks that way."

"The Moon said the same thing," says Dragonfly with a small chuckle as he looks toward the Sun that is now halfway beneath the western horizon.

The Sun also laughs, soft and barely heard above all the sounds of nature and echoes throughout everyone.

"I know," says the Sun. "Who do you think she heard it from?"

Dragonfly raises one eye, lowers the other, smirks, and lets out a gentle laugh.

In that moment, he turns his sight north, as the last light of the Sun dips beneath the horizon.

'Dragonfly Saga: Part I' Continues in 'Tale of Dragonfly Book II: Autumn to Winter'

EPILOGUE

"Dear Traveler, that is an excellent question. Perhaps my favorite you have asked thus far. Why do I tell stories and why have I immersed myself within them?

I suppose I would tell you it is because through time, travel and experience I have come to believe in the simple truth that what lasts forever are children and stories; and I have come to believe in this truth because my own beloved children have been taken from me, due to my holding on to my attachments and comforts—and hiding in the darkness for too long."

Eventually, I learned from the mistakes of my past, found my way out of the shadows; and I found the gift of the present within, and out, onto the illuminated path of creating a brighter future. I survived my self by continuing onward; and I revealed a great gift that is beyond only imagination and just logic.

However, and heed this, Traveler: There was and is a price. There is always a price of equal exchange, something great was lost and something great was found; something given, something taken—and vice versa.

My children have been lost to me for now, and it is a very real possibility that I may never see them again for the rest of my current lifetime; but I still have the truth of the stories and the power to create more.

To answer your question in full, Traveler, I tell the truth of these stories here and now, for my children, and you, to learn from my mistakes and failures; in hopes they may find their way to me, if they wish it. By the power of my word, my voice, and the eternal power of story.

Perhaps, if you listen deeply enough, you may find the present—and the gift—from within the shadows and find your own way to a life without suffering.

You see, Traveler, this is a cautionary tale—and I am its Storyteller."

NOTES

*Cherokee Nation "Two Wolves" Story (Amended), pg. 16.

*Skinner, Charles M. *Myths and Legends of Our Own Land* (Philadelphia: J.B. Lippincott Company, 1896), pg. 16, 37, 44, 45, 47, 57, 63, 69, 70, 76, 92, 100.

*Zen and Taoist Proverbs, pg. 67, 68.

*Blackfoot Proverb, pg. 84.

*Blackfoot Proverb by Chief Crowfoot, pg. 100.

Myths and Legends of Our Own Land by Charles M Skinner is found in the Public Domain and it is written the following: *"This work has been selected by scholars as being culturally important and is part of the knowledge base of civilizations as we know it. This work is in the public domain in the United States of America, and possibly other nations. Within the United States, you may freely copy and distribute this work, as no entity (individual or corporate) has a copyright on the body of the work."*

ABOUT THE AUTHOR

Shane Curtis Fike

A US Army Combat Veteran that served in Operation Iraqi Freedom from 2003-2005, now a published author, Founder and President of The Majesty Foundation Inc., a registered charity for advancing mental health, a Breath Coach, Qigong Teacher, and Daoist Priest-In-Training. For more information and to listen to Shane perform stories as a storyteller visit his linktree and YouTube channel: https://linktr.ee/shanecurtisfike

ABOUT THE ARTIST

Polia Giannoulidis

Polia Giannoulidis is an Abstract Artist who works with water-based mediums, a Graphic Designer/Video Editor and Publisher.

As an artist, Polia uses her creative expression to outwardly showcase her internal matrices of thoughts and emotions. As within, so without. Her body of work focuses on transformation at a cellular level, marrying a higher expressed emotion with a positive thought to activate change. This is then brought to life through the 'wand' of her paint brush.

Together with her husband, Shane, they co-founded the publishing company 'Nox Arcanum Experiment' and a non-profit, 501(c)(3) registered charity organization, The Majesty Foundation Inc. whose mission is to heal trauma and suffering in order to advance mental health by utilizing art and storytelling as healing, living well, and as a means to raise funds and awareness for those in need of mental health services.

The work found within these pages are a visual translation of the messages held within the stories of each chapter.

Everything is energy and has a unique vibratory frequency that can be accessed and understood through deeper levels of consciousness.

When working with clients, intuition and intention are the keys needed to bring through an individual's unique codes, and/or the essence of their business. These codes are language recognized by the soul and represented by the intersecting lines of sacred geometry and the shapes of known and unknown symbols that form Sigils.

Where to find, follow, and contact Polia Giannoulidis:
polia@cosmiccodingdesigns.com
Instagram:
@polia_giannoulidis.art – Artwork

@cosmic.coding – Designs

A Cosmic Odyssey

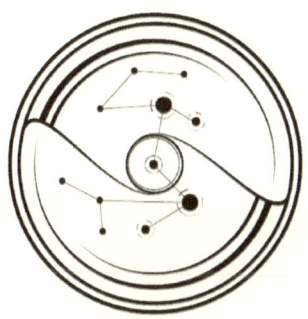

"In the pathway of the Sun,
In the footsteps of the breeze,
Where the world and sky are one,
He shall ride the silver seas,
He shall cut the glittering wave.
I shall sit at home, and rock,
Brew my tea, and snip my thread,
Bleach the linen for my bed,
They will call him brave."
-Penelope (from Homer's Odyssey)

Shane and Polia are star-crossed lovers reliving the ballad of the ages in modern times in extreme polarity. Shane wanders the lands of the North Americas of the United States, adventuring and traversing peril upon his journey inward and outward, though trapped from making his way to his love. While Polia waits and journeys her own inward trek through mind and spirit, nearly ten thousand miles apart in the Southern Hemisphere of that wild land, Australia.

Through space, time, and distance, these two lovers grow in love and endeavor together to create great works from within and throughout the great work. Ever moving onward toward the day, they shall be united for that very first time, embracing one another skin to skin, in that electrifying touch of lips. A kiss that sparks the creation of universes.